HOT COPY

Rachel Vincer

Copyright © 1992 Pam Hanson and Barbara Andrews and
Carol Fox Thomas
Cover Art Copyright © 1992 William Graf

All rights reserved.

No part of this book may be reproduced without written
permission. No part of this book may be transmitted in any form or by any means, electronic
or mechanical, including photocopying, recording, or by
any information storage and retrieval system, without the publisher's
written permission. For information, write to: Meteor
Publishing Corporation, ...

A KISMET® Romance

METEOR PUBLISHING CORPORATION
Bensalem, Pennsylvania

For David, with the power to charm.
And also to C. DeB. for a great European tour.

RACHEL VINCER

Rachel Vincer confesses to being an unregenerate romantic who loves music, reading and traveling to exotic places looking for stories and inspiration. After a childhood spent in India and England, she now makes her home in Toronto, but considers the world her oyster.

ONE

"All reporters are scum. You should know how I feel by now, Tony."

Myles Hunter rose abruptly and walked over to the French windows to stare out into the lush garden. His hand clutched the cellular phone so tightly that the knuckles whitened, but he kept his voice even. Experience had taught him to maintain a facade of control.

"You had your way about that on the last tour," said Tony, undeterred, "and look what almost happened—"

"You've made your point," he cut his manager off impatiently. One more disaster like that and he could kiss ten years of hard work goodbye. What did they say? You're only as good as your last album. He burned with a sudden surge of anger that made him clamp his teeth painfully together in the effort to control himself. "So when am I to expect this . . . this . . . Kate O'Brien." He almost spit out her name, as if it were a four-letter word.

"Noon."

Myles glanced at his watch. "It's eleven-thirty already. Couldn't you have given me any more warning?"

7

Tony chuckled. "If I'd given you more warning you'd have found some urgent reason to be elsewhere."

Myles grimaced. Tony knew him much too well. "Well, I'll see her. But I'm not promising you anything."

"That's all I want. Just hear her out. If I didn't think this would be good for the album . . . for you . . ."

"I know, I know. You've only got my best interests at heart." He said it cynically, but he knew it was true.

Myles switched off the phone and stood staring into the garden. His gaze drifted absently over the clusters of brilliant blue delphiniums lining the cobbled path that led into an artful wilderness of dappled shade. How he hated the idea of yet another reporter trying to pull him to pieces and see what made him tick.

The leafy country lane gradually dwindled down to an unpaved track that ended at a five-barred gate. An hour late already. *Damn*. Kate leaned both arms on the wheel and blew an errant strand of hair away from her flushed, damp face.

The navy linen suit that seemed such a good idea this morning when it was cool and overcast now stuck uncomfortably to her back. She looked down at her crushed and wrinkled skirt and groaned. What a way to make a good impression—assuming she ever got there.

And what had happened to the temperate English springtime? It felt as hot and steamy as Toronto in July. The gears ground in protest as she threw the car into reverse and made a three point turn, then headed back to the last crossroads between tall hedgerows covered in fragrant, creamy blossoms.

For the hundredth time she cursed the paranoia of the famous. Why did Myles Hunter have to play lord of the manor hidden away in darkest Hampshire? Perfect, of course, for a celebrity so jealous of his privacy, especially when it came to the press.

But on his last tour three years ago, he wouldn't let

a reporter anywhere near him, and it had come close to being a failure. A lot was riding on this new album. She was willing to bet he was getting heavy pressure from his record company and his manager, Tony Scott, to be more visible. That's why he'd been giving her this runaround for the last two weeks, putting her off and canceling appointments, until finally Tony suggested she beard him in his den.

She couldn't really blame him for being so elusive. It must get a bit much, being dogged by reporters, not to mention his hysterically devoted fans.

And they'd really have to be devoted to track him down in this rural wilderness. She geared down and swerved hard to the left to avoid a man-eating pothole.

If you weren't a hysterical fan before, you certainly would be after trying to find this guy. Kate giggled at the thought of legions of giddy teenage girls, doomed to wander the maze of hedgerowed lanes forever. She shook her head. Perhaps she'd seen the clay feet of too many idols, but she could never imagine behaving like that kind of a fool over anybody.

Well . . . not now. Not at the mature age of twenty-seven. She squirmed uncomfortably in the black leather bucket seat, vividly recalling herself at seventeen, at Myles Hunter's first concert in Canada. Pushing her way through the crowd to the stage barrier, she had stood with tears streaming down her face, staring up at her idol, not more than ten feet away.

Kate turned back onto the main road and put the pedal to the floor for a moment. This was silly, speeding up wasn't going to help her distance herself from that humiliating memory.

Put those thoughts out of your head, Kate. She couldn't allow her past foibles to rattle her like this. Easing off on the accelerator, she gripped the wheel more firmly. The assignment was too important to *MusicBeat*, and to her career.

Besides, she'd be damned if she'd fulfill Bob's cynical prediction, bridling all over again as she thought of the warning in her editor's gravelly voice.

"I haven't had one female reporter through here who didn't have trouble coping with the business. Either they run a mile the first time someone makes a pass at them or they drool like some idiot groupie and ask stupid questions about clothes."

The sexist pig. She'd show him.

But already she could feel her stomach tightening with nerves. The usual preinterview tension was overlaid with an excitement that had everything to do with meeting Myles Hunter. Well, she couldn't allow herself to be intimidated. No matter how stupid her adolescent crush had been, it was ancient history now.

Mind you, he wasn't just another brainless musician. His lyrics revealed a keen intelligence, and the interviews given before his cold war with the press began had shown him to be bright and articulate. Would she be able to conduct herself like an intelligent woman or be reduced to a blithering idiot?

Oh, God, please don't let me make a fool of myself. When Bob told her about the article covering the comeback tour, she'd felt a quiver of unprofessional anticipation. She reached over, picked up the small CD case from the seat beside her, and glanced at the cover photo.

Myles Hunter stared back at her in shades of gray, sombre and alone. Wearing a loosely cut dark suit, he stood leaning against a Gothic archway.

In the video age you didn't reach his level of fame on mere talent alone. Although he had talent in abundance. But teenage girls around the world didn't buy his posters because of that. Her mouth twisted cynically as she tossed the CD back on the seat.

It was his cool, aristocratically handsome face and supremely elegant personal style, so distinctive in the rough-and-tumble of pop music. Hard to believe he grew up poor and hungry in the toughest part of East End London.

Yet she couldn't label him a poseur, even if he did play the well-bred part to the hilt. After all, image counted for so much these days. And after being a star for ten years, she could hardly call him a flash in the pan.

But now she was late, and the star would not be pleased. He might not even see her at all, and then there'd be hell to pay when Bob found out.

Cresting a hill, the rolling countryside suddenly spread out clearly before her, and she saw it. The mellow red brick of the Georgian manor house nestled timelessly into the rich green hills rising behind. Drowsing in the warm sunshine, it must have looked just like this for the past two hundred springs.

Kate gave a sigh of relief and drove downhill as quickly as possible, stopping at the closed iron gates to identify herself over the intercom while the camera above surveyed her. An old brown Mini sat on the grass verge across the road and she noticed the driver loading a camera equipped with a huge telephoto lens.

Obviously a stringer for one of the national rags. What a loathsome job, hanging around celebrities waiting to catch them off guard. They couldn't pay her enough to do a job like that. As the gates clicked open, she got back in the car and drove up an avenue of ancient yews to the graveled forecourt fronting the house.

As she walked up the shallow marble steps she squared her shoulders, firming her resolve. Grasping the brass ring defiantly, she let it fall three times. Myles Hunter might be a fanatically private person with delusions of grandeur, but he wouldn't be the first, or last, celebrity she'd ever meet.

Kate fought down the sick churning in her stomach,

determined to preserve her self-respect. Besides, he would probably turn out to be an egotistical jerk, like so many of them, and then she'd have no trouble maintaining her perspective.

After several moments she knocked again. Where was everybody? They knew she'd arrived, someone had opened the gate. Another minute went by with no answer. She tapped her foot impatiently on the marble step. Enough was enough. She was late already. Perhaps there was another entrance around the side.

She stepped back and inspected the front of the house, noticing a gate in the high privet hedge bordering the gravel drive. *Well, Alice . . . there's your rabbit hole.*

Myles Hunter glanced up from his book and tensed at the sight of the slender young woman in a navy suit walking boldly along the path leading to his library. Must be that damn reporter finally. She had a lot of nerve, waltzing in uninvited. But what else did he expect?

He stood up from his shady seat on the stone bench and cautiously approached the main path. Peering around the large rhododendron bush, he saw her pause uncertainly outside the French doors of his library. What the hell was she up to?

His mouth set in a grim line. He had to cooperate with the press this time. It was good business, or so Tony kept telling him. But that didn't mean he had to like it. He'd been their victim long enough. His life had been shattered when Alison died, and then they'd compounded the agony with their obscene accusations that he couldn't even refute.

Now it was time to get his own back. And this brazen little fly would be very sorry she ever wandered into his web. With any luck he'd make her so sorry she'd buzz back to her editor and refuse to do the story.

Perhaps it was time to live up to the reputation that scandal-mongering rabble had bestowed on him. If they wanted a depraved sexual animal, then he would give them one, in spades.

He watched as she looked around, her chestnut hair swinging silkily against her shoulders. From where he stood he couldn't see her face, but he couldn't help noticing the feminine curve of her hips and the long shapely length of her legs beneath the brief navy skirt.

He watched her hesitate, then with a quick backward glance at the wild lushness of the garden, she stepped in through the open doors. He smiled with grim satisfaction and followed.

Kate's gaze swept over the beautiful proportions of the spacious high-ceilinged room, sunshine pouring in through a series of French windows. Floor-to-ceiling bookshelves covered every available wall. She shouldn't be in here, but how could she resist? After all, the doors were standing wide open and she only wanted a quick look.

Everything intensified the dreamlike quality of this moment. The scent of roses wafting in from the wild English garden, the drowsy stillness of the afternoon, broken only by the occasional buzzing of a bee. Being in Myles Hunter's library, like Beauty wandering into the enchanted garden of the Beast.

Kate felt a premonitory shiver. She had no business being here and she'd better get out before she got caught. A soft footstep behind her made her stiffen. Too late. She closed her eyes. *Kate. Will you never learn?*

She turned, prepared to do some fast explaining, and felt as if the breath had been knocked out of her body.

He stood framed in the doorway, the brilliant afternoon sun turning his blond hair to spun gold, his gray eyes boring into hers, a shocked expression in their smoky depths.

My God, he's gorgeous.

Kate stood gaping at him. It wasn't as if she didn't know what to expect. She'd seen his face a thousand times, but here, in this idyllic quiet, with no stage lights, no milling fans, she'd been jolted by a gut reaction that took her completely by surprise.

Realizing her mouth was still hanging open, she clamped it shut. What on earth could she possibly say to get herself out of this one?

Nothing had prepared Myles for the impact of those huge ingenuous green eyes as they gazed back at him. He felt the long-dormant unfurling of desire as his eyes skimmed the soft pink lower lip that trembled ever so slightly.

Was he mad? How could he forget, even for a second, who she was and why she was here? Ignoring that tantalizing quiver, he stepped into the room with renewed determination to teach her a lesson. He quelled the urge to laugh out loud. Now he knew what they meant by sweet revenge.

Kate took an involuntary step back. Away from the dangerous gleam in Myles Hunter's eyes as he advanced toward her.

"I . . . I'm sorry," she stammered. "The door was open and . . ."

"You don't have to explain," he cut in. His cultured English accent held an insinuating undertone that made the hairs at her nape prickle and stand on end. "I admire your tenacity; not many of my fans find their way this far."

"I think you misunderstand Mr. Hunter, I'm . . ."

"Please, let's not spoil this with talk." His eyes burned a slow path over her trembling body and Kate backed away, feeling awkward and embarrassed by his behavior as he continued bearing down on her. "I know why you're here and I'm flattered."

Her clammy hands clutched her bag like a shield across her breasts. She felt ridiculous, like the timid heroine in a silent movie. In her wildest imaginings she'd never pictured suave, devastatingly handsome Myles Hunter behaving like a lecherous satyr. She felt sick with disillusionment.

How could she have spun all those overblown romantic fantasies about this degenerate reptile? She'd never believed those newspaper stories about his orgiastic exploits, until now. And to think she had worried about behaving like some lovestruck teenybopper. She shuddered. This had gone far enough. "Mr. Hunter, I'm not who you think I am," she protested as he continued bearing down on her, backing her into the corner until she felt the hard edge of his desk against the back of her thighs. He had her trapped, and she didn't like the salacious gleam in his eyes.

"It doesn't matter. Such devotion deserves to be rewarded." He smiled. That famous smile. Kate felt disoriented, something was terribly wrong with this picture.

Panic-stricken, she dropped her bag and gripped the edge of the desk as his hands came down on either side of her and he leaned forward, his body mere inches from touching hers.

His gray eyes bored into hers as his face came closer. This couldn't be happening to her. What was she going to do? She could feel the heat of his body, could smell his subtle, spicy aftershave.

She was practically lying on his desk, her feet barely touching the floor; if he came any closer she'd be flat on her back and he'd be on top of her, on that book-strewn surface. She held her breath.

Then suddenly he straightened and stepped away.

Where moments before his eyes had been glazed with ardor, now they were cool and impassive.

"You *are* Kate O'Brien, I presume?"

His unemotional words were like a slap in the face. "What?" she gasped, sliding down off the desk and struggling to get her bearings.

"You've already kept me waiting close to two hours. Do you mind if we get on with this?"

"Not till you explain to me what that was all about!" she demanded. His stunning reversal from stalking lothario to grim iceman left her completely bewildered.

"Well, isn't that what you lot expect from me? Besides, I might ask what you were doing in my library."

Her self-righteous anger sputtered and died at the awful reminder that she had been trespassing. She stumbled through a shamefaced attempt to explain. "Well, nobody answered my knock. I just thought I'd go round to . . . the . . . The door was open and . . ."

"And like all the rest of your kind you couldn't resist the urge to snoop." His voice was like sand on velvet, and as cold as a winter's night. "This is a private house, not a peep show for the benefit of the press."

His cutting tone made her bristle, despite her sense of guilt. Yet she felt much too conscious of the physical awareness vibrating within her, the racing heartbeat, the burning imprint where his body had almost touched hers that she'd carry around with her till the day she died. Kate choked back a giggle. She must have really lost it if she was starting to think in fan magazine drivel. And how could she even contemplate laughing at a time like this?

It had to be the most calamitous goof she'd ever made. Worse than the time Sister Mary Jane walked into the middle of a cafeteria food fight just as Kate let fly a gooey chocolate-covered doughnut. And somehow this time she didn't think she'd get away with just a month of detentions.

"I'm sorry," she replied with all the quiet dignity she could muster.

"You mean you're sorry you were caught."

Who did he think he was, talking to her like that? There was no need for him to take this cynical tone with her; he'd known who she was all along. If she'd been wrong in trespassing, he'd been equally wrong staging that little scene to frighten her off. Well, he wouldn't find it easy. Whatever it took, she'd get the story. Even if it meant eating crow.

Swallowing her resentment, Kate picked up her purse and straightened her jacket. Myles took his seat behind the desk, waving her to the wing chair across from him.

That famous face stared back at her, grim and more than a little hostile. A stray shaft of sunlight gleamed on the pale-blond hair, worn short and brushed back, just touching his collar, contrasting sharply with the loose black shirt and trousers. Deep-gray eyes bored into her implacably, so familiar and yet unfamiliar.

He looked older than the image she had in her mind, his features less soft, more defined. Not merely attractive but compelling. It gave her the strangest sensation seeing him here in the flesh.

Why hadn't he just kicked her out for snooping? Whatever the reason, she had to take advantage of her good fortune and try to salvage something out of the mess she'd created. *Calm down, pull yourself together and pretend that fiasco never happened.*

"I'm sorry I was late, I got lost . . ."

"I assumed there must be some good reason." The overt anger in his voice had subsided to a precise, dry sarcasm. "Tony told me you were given directions; obviously they were not explicit enough."

"No, quite frankly they were completely inadequate." Her unfamiliarity with the twisted maze of roads crisscrossing the English countryside had made a mockery of his manager's directions. Kate fought down the urge to argue. She'd been given a second chance and couldn't let his antagonism goad her into another mistake.

"Your colleague at the gate somehow managed to find his way here."

"I don't consider a tabloid stringer my colleague," she shot back. He merely lifted an eyebrow at her defensiveness, then his gaze wandered over her in cool appraisal.

Kate sat in the wing chair, gripping the black velvet arms tightly. Willing herself to stay cool, she faced him squarely over the expanse of the Chippendale desk.

Myles sat back, sinking into the luxurious upholstery, his elbows on the arms of his chair, chin resting on the tent of his clasped fingers. He looked very blond against the black leather, and very handsome.

Pinning her with a penetrating gray gaze, he made her feel disturbingly self-conscious. Yet she sensed something indefinable beneath the cool surface besides anger.

"Before we go any further, I want you to know I'm completely opposed to this idea."

No kidding! Why else would she have come all the way down to this godforsaken spot?

"However, Tony persuaded me to hear you out before I make a decision," he continued, picking up the gold pen lying on the desk and playing with it absently.

Kate took a deep breath. Now was the time for diplomacy, or she could kiss the story goodbye. She found herself watching his long fingers and well-shaped hands with unwilling fascination. Artist's hands. She lifted her gaze to meet the shrewd gray gleam in his eyes.

"All right, Miss O'Brien." He leaned back again with a cynical tilt of his head. "What makes *your* approach so different."

He had his nerve, acting as if she'd come cap in hand for a favor. He stood to gain as much, or more than the magazine. But despite the provocation, she couldn't give in to her annoyance. She had to convince him. Be reassuring.

"I know why you don't want to be interviewed and I understand . . ." Kate began, launching into her semi-rehearsed speech. He lifted a sardonic eyebrow and she faltered, then tried again. "You're thinking I would say that anyway, but . . ."

"So you can read my mind. What a useful talent for someone in your line of work." His chilling smile was disquieting. "So much easier than scavenging through your victim's garbage or spying on them with telephoto lenses . . . But I forgot, you don't bother being so circumspect. What's your forte? Breaking and entering?" His voice hardened. "And, of course, if all else fails, what you don't know you can always just make up."

Kate stiffened. Walking into his library uninvited had been wrong, but she'd apologized, why did he have to keep going on about it? And why was she getting *so angry*?

Because he's dented your female ego, Kate. That's why. He hadn't shown the tiniest hint of response to her femininity, and she was ashamed to admit it, but it galled her. And that ridiculous Don Juan act had been the crowning insult.

She stopped, took a deep breath, and got a grip on her temper, silently lecturing herself. She came here to get a story, and by God she was going to get one. She couldn't let her wounded pride and his arrogance stand in her way.

"Mr. Hunter," she began, "I understand your objection to being interviewed. You've had more than your share of rough treatment by the press." Seeing an angry flicker in his eyes, she went on hurriedly. "But neither I nor my magazine are interested in a sensational exposé of your personal life. We want to do a serious article on your upcoming tour. Give our readers a feel for the massive effort that's involved behind the scenes.''

Kate paused, hoping she saw a shade less anger and suspicion in his steady, unblinking gaze. It was unnerving, and she felt as if she were beginning to babble. He uncoiled out of the chair with an easy suppleness, striding over to the window hands in pockets. Standing with his back to her, he stared out at the garden, apparently deep in thought.

Kate slumped back into the chair, realizing every muscle in her body had been poised with tension. Now that she wasn't the focus of his critical gaze, she could indulge her desire to study him more closely.

He stood just over six feet tall, his leanness making him look even taller. The simple but expensive clothes hung on his athletic frame in a way that made it impossible not to speculate about the broad shoulders and narrow hips beneath. He moved with an animal grace, hinting at a firm muscularity at odds with the aristocratic image.

In her naive youth he'd been her idea of the perfect man. If anything, he was even more attractive at thirty-six. She had made the mistake of commenting to her editor on how well he had aged and remembered Bob's disgruntled answer: ''If I had his money, I would, too.'' Kate clamped a hand over her mouth, stifling the sudden, subversive urge to laugh. No amount of money could ever have transformed short, chubby, balding Bob Hutchinson into Myles Hunter.

Myles turned his head. ''Care to share the joke?'' He did not look amused.

She mumbled something incoherent. He shot her a disdainful look before turning back to his abstracted pondering, leaving her to continue trying to make sense of the enigma he presented.

Ever since she had turned to see him standing in the

library doorway, she'd been physically aware of him in a way that disturbed her.

She'd met many famous, attractive men, but had never had any problem maintaining the calm detachment she prided herself on. It accounted for her professional approach to a subject that so often lent itself to gossipy drivel.

But this was different. It had only been an adolescent crush, but everything about him—his looks, his style—had always appealed very deeply. Now here he was in the flesh. Not some magazine-cover icon or a flickering screen image. A living, breathing man, whose tangible masculine presence evoked an answering feminine response in her. It was appalling to realize that finding him a cold, manipulative egotist didn't completely obliterate the attraction.

Suddenly Myles rounded on her with an air of challenge. "Why do *you* want to do this story?"

She returned his gaze with equal boldness, refusing to be cowed. "Because it will sell magazines. A lot of fans out there would be interested to know what goes on behind the scenes."

"And you'll just be writing about the tour? No tawdry personal muckraking?"

Why did he have to phrase it like that? Kate took a deep breath. Now it came down to the crunch. "And, of course, I'll need an in-depth interview. Your fans are interested in what you have to say."

For one long, suspense-filled moment he said nothing. Tony had warned her this would be her biggest obstacle.

"They can listen to the music. No one needs to know anything else." His patrician features remained impassive.

"I'm not talking about personal information. Just some insight into how you function as an artist."

"I'll have to think about it."

That wasn't good enough. He could be thinking

about it for six months and the tour would be over. She had to gamble on pushing him a little harder.

"Well . . . let me put it this way. Either you give me an interview or I'll just have to write the article from my point of view. Okay, so you don't like what's written about you. Here's your opportunity to refute all that. If you don't take it, you only have yourself to blame."

"Are you threatening me, Miss O'Brien?" His voice held an undertone of cool menace.

"I want this story, Mr. Hunter. Would I be stupid enough to threaten you?" Kate met his uncompromising gaze head-on, refusing to be intimidated.

He turned back to his contemplation of the garden. Dense silence filled the room. She heard bees droning outside as a clock ticked off the minutes in the drowsy sunshine.

Her gaze wandered over the crowded bookshelves, looking for clues to unravel the mystery of this complex, fascinating man. Over the years she'd created an image of him, pieced together from her own interpretation of his lyrics and the rare interviews with him she'd seen. Now here she was, facing this absolute stranger who bore no resemblance to the Myles Hunter of her imagination, and she felt disoriented and, more unreasonably, disappointed.

One thing was certain. He presented a challenging puzzle. Why on earth did he have to be so damned infuriating?

But she couldn't deny that the prospect of touring Europe, and perhaps coming to understand him better in the process, presented an intriguing combination.

He turned back, catching her off guard as she tried to read book titles across the room.

"All right. You can do the story on the tour. I haven't decided about the personal interview yet. *But*,

I want final approval of everything before publication," he insisted.

"Well . . . that's not the usual thing." He didn't want much, did he?

"Look, it's my only condition, but it's not negotiable." His mouth became grim again.

"I've already given you my assurance I won't be taking a personal angle in this story." Kate felt honorbound to hold out for her journalistic freedom, but something told her she'd never win this particular fight. Besides, Bob wouldn't thank her if she lost the story through pure stubbornness.

"I've learned not to take assurances at face value," he said tersely. "Especially where the press is concerned."

Kate tried to check her rising anger. Why was she letting him get under her skin like this? She shouldn't take it personally. After all, he hadn't exactly been treated with kid gloves.

She thought of the clipping files she'd combed through, preparing for the assignment. All the lurid tabloid headlines from four years ago about his wife and all the women he had flaunted under her nose. She despised that kind of yellow journalism. His suspicion was understandable.

"I hope I can do something to change your opinion of us. In the meantime, I'm sure I can persuade my editor to accept that condition." She couldn't hide her reluctance.

He nodded in apparent tacit agreement, marking the end of the interview. Kate rose and approached him. Any hope of getting things on a better footing between them would obviously rest with her. It took a lot to shake her self-possession, but he had done it. Never in the course of her job had anyone managed to humiliate her so completely, and she only had herself to blame.

"I'll look forward to working with you." She extended her hand with a conciliatory smile, hoping in vain for some answering warmth of response. He hesitated, then took her hand with a firm, smooth grip.

"You won't regret your decision, you know." She casually but quickly disengaged her hand. What was the matter with her? It was only a handshake. He'd done worse. "Besides, as Mr. Scott pointed out, this will be good publicity before the American leg of the tour. And what's wrong with a little free publicity?" She tried to infuse her voice with optimism.

He tightened his firm, sensual mouth in the semblance of a smile. "If there's one thing I've learned in my long, checkered career . . . it's that absolutely nothing is free."

"You've got to learn to trust people occasionally." *Good grief, Kate. What next? Your rendition of "The Good Ship Lollipop?"* Myles raised an incredulous eyebrow. "Well, that's a very touching sentiment. Forgive me if I reserve judgment for now."

His eyes stared down into hers, calm and cool. Kate met them with a challenge, a shred of defiance still lingering. *Now don't start a debate on professional integrity..* No matter how much his attitude irked her, she had to be content with his qualified agreement.

"I'll see you to your car."

Now she was being dismissed, his distasteful obligation concluded. Kate couldn't help feeling relieved as he stepped aside, ushering her through the double doors standing opposite the portals of disaster through which she'd entered.

He led her into a spacious hall tiled in black-and-white marble and Kate looked around in awe. The house lived up to the promise of its exterior, a beautiful example of classical purity. Tall, elegant windows framed the entrance and flooded the pale, airy foyer in reflected light. The regal sweep of a broad staircase led the eye up to a high, plastered ceiling.

One of the doors on her left stood slightly ajar, and

as they walked by Kate couldn't resist craning her neck for a peek. She caught a glimpse of Persian carpets on polished boards, dusty Wedgwood-green-and-white walls, perfectly proportioned Regency simplicity that took her breath away.

"I thought my little masquerade would have cured you of your reckless propensity to snoop."

The displeasure in his voice made her tense. "I'm sorry you see it that way. I was just admiring your beautiful home." She risked a glance at him and was not reassured by the cynical twist of his mouth.

Silently he opened the front door, ushering her through, and she found herself once more at the graveled court.

"The tour starts in Brussels, two weeks from now. Tony will get in touch with you about all the details, the travel schedule and so on."

Kate nodded and slid into her small red two-seater, just as she noticed a figure down at the end of the drive, outside the gate. The sun glinted on something in his hands.

"Smile . . . You're having your picture taken."

She looked up at Myles for a moment in confusion. Of course. The tabloid photographer. After saying goodbye with stiff politeness, she drove off through the rustling archway of trees. Slowing down as the gates opened before her, she noticed the brown Mini disappearing up the road.

In her rearview mirror she saw Myles standing in the courtyard watching her. *Probably making sure I've left the premises*. Her mouth compressed humorlessly.

He watched the red car turn and disappear.

Why had he agreed to let her come? He could have justifiably insisted on another reporter being assigned to the article. But he had to admit a reluctant admiration for the way she had rallied, in spite of his deliberate attempt to scare her off. Her tenacity impressed him.

That was the reason. It had nothing to do with that wild impulse he had felt when he had her trapped against his desk. The impulse to find out if those lips felt as soft and kissable as they looked. He'd almost fallen for that provocative, wide-eyed appeal. Damn it! Why had he agreed to let her come? That woman spelled trouble.

Kate let out her breath with a long sigh and reflected on the interview as she drove slowly back up the winding road. It occurred to her that Myles was unique. Most of the musicians she saw would do anything for publicity, especially with a career apparently on a downswing. Insisting on personal privacy like that was a risky stand to take.

As she got onto the motorway, speeding up to join the stream of traffic, she couldn't help wondering why. Why had he agreed to her coming on the tour?

Country gave way to suburbs, rapidly getting denser as she approached London. Navigating the tortured knots of city traffic, she couldn't shake off her unease over the attraction she felt for him.

It had to be just a temporary aberration, left-over teenage lust burning itself out. It had *better* have burned itself out by the time she saw him again. Because the alternative didn't bear thinking about.

TWO

"You're going to Europe with Myles Hunter! You lucky girl."

Her sister's voice sounded far away. Kate could well imagine the whole deep Atlantic that lay between them.

"Don't get too excited, Maggie." She wedged the phone between shoulder and ear. "He thinks reporters are something that crawl out from under a rock." Kate continued sorting her research notes. The stacks of photocopies and index cards almost covered her desk in the tiny living room of the borrowed flat.

"So, come on. Tell me. Is he as gorgeous in person or do they airbrush all his pictures? If you tell me he's old and fat now, I'll just die."

Kate had to laugh at the theatrical anguish in her older sister's voice. "Quite the contrary. Considering the pitfalls of his environment, I'd say he's survived remarkably well. He still looks . . . quite attractive."

A sudden vivid image of him flashed into her mind. Framed in the doorway of his library, his virile good looks and potent aura of masculinity bathed in the golden glow of sunlight, like a Greek god just stepped down from Olympus.

27

She shook her head to clear it of the image. *Greek god, Kate? This heat must be affecting your brain*. No wonder she'd been incapable of asserting herself in her usual way. But considering the effect he had on her, and her guilt over intruding, it still amazed her that she'd been able to pull herself together and talk him into letting her do the story.

There was a pause, slightly longer than the usual long-distance delay.

"All right, Kate. Spill the beans. There's more to this than you're admitting." So typical of Maggie to pick up on her slight hesitancy.

"No . . . no, not really." She knew how lame her denial must sound.

"Come on. 'Fess up. It must have been a real thrill to actually meet him."

"It would have been a real thrill if he hadn't been so arrogant and full of himself." She went on to tell Maggie the whole story of their encounter.

Maggie laughed. "Poor baby. He really burst your bubble. How disillusioning. I remember when your room was plastered with his posters and he was all you ever talked about."

"Don't remind me," Kate shuddered. "I guess that's partly what made the interview so difficult. You know, Maggie, I couldn't tell this to anyone else, but, even though he made me so furious, there was still something about him I found awfully distracting. I should have got over that silly hero worship years ago. It was frightening, the way he made me feel. So vulnerable."

"You're human, kiddo. You're not nearly as tough as you like to think you are."

"Yes, but I can't afford to let that kind of thing distract me. You know what it's like for women in this business. It's an uphill battle to be taken seriously."

"Look, honey, you know you're a good reporter. Don't let this undermine your confidence. After all, it's not every day a woman meets her hero and finds him a complete jerk. Even if he is a cute, sexy jerk," Maggie finished with an encouraging laugh.

Kate felt cheered up, in spite of herself. "Yes, but of all the men in the world, why Myles Hunter? I have to follow him around Europe for three weeks. I guess I'm lucky he treated me like pond scum. If he turned his charm on me, I could make a real fool of myself."

"If he did turn his charm on you, he'd be doing himself a favor."

"Thanks, but I'm not interested in being the flavor of the month, and that's all men like him are into. Besides . . ." Kate laughed, "I think there's a union rule. You have to be an actress or a model, and drop-dead gorgeous to boot. That hardly describes me, does it?"

"Don't sell yourself short. You're a very pretty girl. Any man would be lucky to have you," Maggie said loyally, "including Myles Hunter."

"Thanks for the ego boost Mags, but there's no danger of that. He's just an assignment."

"Does that mean you're still sticking to the no-men rule?" Her sister changed tack.

"I am not avoiding men," Kate replied with tired patience. "You know that perfectly well. Just men in the music business." She must have told Maggie how she felt about a million times by now.

"Just who else are you going to meet in your job?" Maggie persisted. "You know Kate, they can't all be depraved maniacs. Some of them must be normal. Maybe Myles Hunter will get over his snit and turn out to be pretty nice."

"*Forget* about Myles Hunter. He has delusions of godhood and I'm not interested in worshipping at his shrine."

Kate smiled at Maggie's throaty chuckle and swiftly changed the subject to ask about Eric and the boys.

Soon Maggie was regaling her with hilarious stories of the unexpected havoc two-year-old twins could wreak.

At length Kate put down the phone with a sigh. Leaning her chin on her hand, she stared out the window of the small Chelsea flat with a sudden stab of unexpected homesickness.

In the park across the road, a blanket of bluebells rippled and shimmered beneath the trees in the breezy spring sunshine. Back home, everyone would still be praying they'd seen the last snow flurry of the winter. No, it wasn't for the weather she yearned. But how she wished herself back in Maggie's kitchen, in her small house in the suburbs of Toronto, having a good sisterly chat. It had been months since her last trip home. The transfer from New York had happened too quickly to permit even a flying visit.

Maggie was the one person in the world Kate could tell absolutely anything and know she'd understand. But it just wasn't the same over the phone. Maybe because they were only fifteen months apart, she and Maggie were closer than most sisters, although their paths in life couldn't have been more different.

Maggie had followed their mother's route of an early marriage, giving up her job as a nurse to stay at home. With a third child on the way, she seemed completely happy with her role in life.

Kate had never wanted such a circumscribed existence. Her adventurous, inquisitive nature had led her into journalism, a career she loved. But still, she envied her sister's sense of contentment and satisfaction. Did that kind of fulfillment come from being loved? Would *she* ever know that kind of happiness? Looking ahead, Kate wondered rather wistfully what lay there for her.

Why on earth start suddenly thinking along those lines? The last two years had seen her career jumping ahead by leaps and bounds, making her reputation in a competitive business. She hadn't the time or the inclination to become involved with anyone. Besides, she wasn't interested in the shallow, fleeting liaisons so many of her friends took for granted. So why this unexpected feeling of something missing?

It must have been talking to Maggie that set her thinking that way . . . Kate shook her head in irritation and snapped out of the reverie. She took the next folder and slapped it down on the desk. This was no time for getting introspective. She had far too much work to do.

"How much money do you expect to make from this tour, Myles?" a reporter shouted out from the back of the room. From her seat near the front Kate cringed.

Myles Hunter looked taken aback, but rallied quickly, yelling back with a disarming smile, "Not nearly as much as I'd like." A wave of laughter ran through the crowd.

The press conference announcing the tour was being held at the luxurious Connaught hotel in central London. Ever since arriving, Kate had been questioning whether this could possibly be the same man she had seen a week before.

Myles and his manager had entered the room to applause and taken their seats behind the battery of microphones on the long, raised table. Myles's gaze had swept over the room, briefly pausing as it lit on Kate, then coolly moving on. *Looks like I'm still in the deep freeze.*

Tony Scott read out a press release announcing the start of the tour, and said Myles was looking forward to being out on the road again. He then invited questions from the journalists ranged in the rows of chairs filling the small ballroom of the hotel.

While flashbulbs went off incessantly, Kate watched Myles closely. Although the smile never left his face, she sensed a strained quality that told her he wasn't completely at ease, particularly compared to Tony Scott's relaxed good humor.

On meeting his manager a week before, she'd been struck by the contrast between Tony's open friendliness and Myles's daunting introspective reserve. But it was obviously a winning combination because he'd been with Myles from the very start.

Then the questions began and she had listened in amazement. There was no trace of the inner tension she'd sensed earlier. Pleasant and communicative, Myles answered the questions with an articulate charm far removed from his cold hostility toward her.

Was this the man who despised reporters? As far as she could tell, he had them all in the palm of his hand. Only once did he become annoyed.

From the front row a spiky-haired blonde clad in black leather had asked, "It's no secret that the reviews of your last tour were pretty negative. How do you respond to the speculation you'll just be cashing in on the old hits this time, because the new stuff's so gloomy?"

Myles stiffened, his eyes sliding over to Kate for a moment with a look that told her she was no better than that insensitive bitch.

"You're talking about the product of ten years of hard work. I'd hardly call it cashing in. Besides . . ." he turned and looked pointedly at Kate, "I'm only giving my fans what they want."

Just the music, she remembered him saying, *they don't need to know anything else*. She met his eyes. Just beneath the charm she sensed a tired distrust.

"Doesn't the representative from *MusicBeat* have any questions she'd like to direct at me?"

The smile was urbane, but his eyes were hard and critical. She knew he was expecting something equally insensitive from her. Okay, she could play that game.

With deliberate arrogance she leaned back in her chair and crossed her legs.

"Well, you've already been asked about money . . ." The steady gaze of his gray eyes was doing strange things to her pulse rate, but she wouldn't let him intimidate her. "That only leaves one other inflammatory subject: your sex life. Since I don't think you'd satisfy my curiosity about that, I guess I won't bother asking."

The room erupted in laughter at her outrageousness.

Myles had to fight down the urge to smile. One thing he had to say for her, she had spunk. He met the defiance in her eyes and took her measure. He hated spunk.

"Thank you so much for your restraint."

Everyone laughed again, but Kate couldn't miss the light of battle behind that cool, sardonic look. Something inside her stirred and rose to the challenge. His gaze held hers captive and she shivered at the steely determination she saw there. Something told her to be careful. This man wasn't used to losing anything.

She swallowed hard and stared down at her notepad with unseeing eyes. Perhaps this was one challenge she should run from. He wasn't her only adversary, she thought, looking back up to catch his gaze as it lingered on her a few seconds longer. Her biggest adversary might turn out to be herself.

Kate dashed down the boarding ramp and slipped through the opening just before the flight attendant slid the hatch shut with a heavy thunk. Thanks to the motorway traffic, she'd barely made Heathrow in time for the Brussels flight. Why? Why had malevolent fate conspired to make her late again, when she'd been so determined to show herself in a better light to Myles Hunter.

Toward the front of the plane she spotted Tony's curly dark head as he turned around, looked over the back of his headrest, and waved at her. The flight attendant quickly led her to the empty seat beside him, across the aisle from Myles Hunter, who watched her with a cool stare as she hastily buckled the seat belt.

"Lost the airport, did you?" he asked, then turned back to his book, leaving Kate feeling like a scatter-brained idiot, without the wits to muster up a snappy reply.

Luckily the jet engines screamed to life at that moment, making response impossible, and the plane began rumbling along in preparation for take-off.

"We were afraid you weren't going to make it." A friendly smile warmed Tony's brown eyes. He handed her a stack of papers and folders. "I thought we could go over the tour itinerary. I've got some background material for you on all the venues, and press kits from the promoters."

Then he dropped a newspaper on top of the pile on her lap. "Looks like *you* made the headlines for a change." He had a sly grin on his smooth, boyish face.

She looked down at the paper and there they stood. Myles and herself on page 6 of the *News of the Globe*. The caption trumpeted the question, *Myles Hunter's New Mystery Woman?*

"Oh, no," Kate groaned in disbelief, and her eyes slid over to Myles. From across the aisle, he shot her a disdainful look that lumped her right in with the scum who specialized in this trash.

But Tony just laughed. "I don't know, Myles. I'd be flattered to have my name linked with someone as pretty as Kate."

·She smiled back at him self-consciously. But obviously Myles wasn't as bowled over by her charms as Tony. He went back to the book which absorbed his attention, while she tried to concentrate on what his manager was telling her about the tour.

She heard barely one word in ten. When Tony finally closed his thick itinerary and squeezed past her to go to the washroom, she sighed with relief and sank back into her seat, vowing to go over the itinerary sometime when she wasn't a mass of nerves. Every fiber in her body sang with awareness of Myles, less than three feet away.

Straining to look out of the corner of her eye, she could just see his long fingers cradling the book. *Lucky book.* Below the pushed-up sleeves of his white cotton sweater, fine golden hairs covered his forearm and curled around his gold watch band. Kate felt a funny little quiver in the pit of her stomach. She had to be cracking up, if just the sight of his bare arm could do this to her. Especially since the fascination was so one-sided. She could be sitting in that seat stark naked and he'd still have his nose buried in a book. Well, she'd have to do something about that.

"Good book?" she asked, leaning slightly across the aisle.

Myles looked up in surprise. "I doubt if you'd think so." He turned the book so she could see the title: *The Classical Spirit—English Architecture in the Eighteenth Century.* His look told her he clearly thought it beyond her.

"Oh . . . yes. I found it *very* interesting."

Myles raised one eyebrow and slowly closed the book. Kate smiled at his barely concealed skepticism.

He rested his hands on the volume in his lap and turned toward her, nettled by the amusement in her green eyes. "So, tell me. What did you think of . . . the section on Nash's work in Bath?" That would teach her to laugh at him. Let her try and squirm her way out of this one.

"Fascinating . . . but I would have liked to know more about the Gothic Revival country houses he did with Repton."

He stared at her for a full minute, his eyes drawn to the smile quivering on her full, soft lips. It was almost smug. With an effort of will he tore his gaze away from her mouth and met the challenge in her eyes. Damn it, he'd underestimated her. What else had she found out about him, if she'd researched him so well she even knew his taste in reading?

Never mind, he had his own resources. He could pay her back in kind. He *would* pay her back in kind.

"Pardon me if I'm not dazzled by your cleverness. No doubt next you'll be telling me what kind of toothpaste I use."

Kate's amusement faded at his disparaging comment. He thought she was flaunting her knowledge of his personal life. She'd unwittingly made a bad situation even worse. And judging by his stony expression, now was not the time to explain that her brother Sean, the budding architect, was forever passing on books he thought would interest her.

Tony reappeared in the aisle between them and Kate moved to let him back into his seat. She glanced across at Myles, immersed in his book again. He was so impassive, so impenetrable. There was no getting through to him. How was she ever going to break through the restraint between them? Watching him, she mused once again on the discrepancy between his background and his image.

All the biographies were remarkably sketchy and contradictory when it came to his early life, with only one common thread. He had been brought up by his mother alone, in the poorest part of London. Just one faded picture they all seemed to have got hold of. A thin little boy in front of a grim, dingy Victorian school.

It sounded like a deprived, depressing childhood. A far cry from Kate's own happy memories of modest comfort and unstinting love. How to connect that little boy with the reserved man, looking elegantly casual in his white sweater and black close-fitting denims across the aisle from her? How could she ever bridge the distance between them?

And, in spite of his undisguised animosity, it was still there. That uncomfortably heightened physical awareness. Even after the press conference, she had still hoped the effect would wear off. That hope had vanished the moment she set eyes on him again.

But what woman could be immune to his appeal? Her eyes traced his profile, the high cheekbones and firm jawline, lingering on his mouth. Neither full nor thin, the finely carved masculine line of his lips made her feel like reaching out and tracing them with her fingertip.

A vicarious thrill shot through her, making her lean her head back and close her eyes. How would it have felt if he had kissed her, when his lips had hovered mere inches from hers on that unforgettable afternoon? She could almost feel the warmth of his strong arms molding her against his lean body, while those wonderful lips clung to hers in a deliciously slow, hotly passionate kiss. The image was so sensual she could feel a wave of heat trembling through her, turning her thighs to jelly, almost as if it were really happening.

With a start, she opened her eyes to find that deepgray enigmatic gaze locked on hers. Kate felt a mortified flush creeping into her cheeks as he held her captive, unable to break away until he looked down again.

Oh, God! *Please don't let him read my mind*. She stared sightlessly at the promotion sheets on the tray in front of her. How could she maintain a shred of professional dignity if he thought she panted after him like so many others?

Women were always throwing themselves at his feet, that was the simple truth. Probably millions of them all over the world would gladly jump into his bed and do anything that took his fancy. And he knew it.

The thought pulled Kate up short. How degrading, to be part of that anonymous crowd of willing female bodies. She could never allow anyone to see her in that light, she vowed with an unconscious lift of her chin. She had too much self-respect.

They were making the approach to Brussels now, as the brief flight neared its end. Kate rebuckled her seat belt with a sense of regaining inner control. As long as she could keep things in perspective, everything would be all right.

Emerging into the arrivals area, they were quickly besieged by a jostling group of reporters.

"Myles! . . . Myles! . . ." they screamed, yelling unintelligible questions and recklessly shoving microphones into his face. Kate struggled to keep her feet and hang on to her bags, buffeted on all sides in the crush.

Like a pack of animals, they kept relentlessly hounding their prey. Myles just gave a strained smile and said nothing as the cameras flashed, while Tony managed to avoid answering anyone directly. Having been part of crowds like that herself, Kate found it unsettling to see it through the eyes of the quarry.

"We'll be seeing you all at the press conference later." Tony flashed an ingratiating grin and waved at the crowd. "But thanks for coming to meet us. . . . That's right, no comment," he replied to the insistent questions.

Kate had to admire the way he maintained his good temper. Nothing seemed to shake him. He and Myles pushed their way through, with Kate in tow, until they reached the Mercedes limousine waiting to take them to a scheduled radio interview.

"See you later," Tony threw back over his shoulder as he got in and Kate hailed a taxi.

Kate leaned her elbows on the windowsill and surveyed the jumbled rooftops of Brussels. Amid the copper green and terracotta red, the plain boxlike lines of modern buildings punctuated the domes and spires of the Old World.

The center of Europe in many ways, Brussels housed the headquarters of NATO and the Common Market. It bustled with a formidable diplomatic bureaucracy. It would be an interesting place to explore, if only they had more than two days.

A knock at the door announced the arrival of room service with her tea. While the waiter rolled in the trolley Kate tuned in the radio station for Myles's interview.

His music filled the room. Against the spare background of bass and drums, he sang of love and longing. That distinctive husky voice with an edge of sadness that touched her irresistibly, intertwining with the sinuous line of the saxophone. Kicking off her shoes, Kate curled up in the comfortable armchair by the window to drink her tea and listen.

She closed her eyes as the music washed over her, letting herself be carried away in its sensual spell. How could she reconcile the distant, arrogant Myles Hunter with the person who could write music and lyrics of such haunting sensitivity and beauty?

As the song ended, the D.J. introduced Myles and began the interview. If she hadn't known the innocuous questions were carefully prescreened, Kate would have sworn his charming, articulate answers were completely off the cuff.

So, the press conference had been no fluke. He seemed to reserve all his hostility toward the press exclusively for her. Yet, despite the way he acted, she couldn't ignore her physical awareness of him. Even now, just hearing his soft, low voice over the radio, she could feel it.

The interview ended, they closed it off with another cut from the album, and the mood changed completely.

Where the first song had been slowly sensual and yearning, now the insistent driving beat throbbed with powerful desire.

She had always reacted to the raw sexual passion in his voice, even before she knew what sex was all about. But now she had met him, and in spite of their ongoing battle and her determination to remain impervious to his appeal, Kate found herself constantly wondering what sort of a lover he would be.

What depths were there under his impassive surface? She shifted in her chair, uncomfortably aware she could never listen to his music in the same way again.

Those were the kind of reactions she'd have to learn to master. She rose quickly, resisting the impulse to change the station, and began unpacking the few things needed for her brief stay.

Now they were playing cuts from his previous album, the one he'd recorded after his wife's tragic death in a car crash. The Sunday papers said she'd found him with another woman and had driven away so distraught that he was as clearly to blame as if he'd driven the car off the bridge himself. No wonder the lyrics were so bleak and hopelessly cynical.

She jumped up and lifted her little portable computer onto the desk, swallowing the hard lump in her throat. She'd heard that song a thousand times, but the words had suddenly taken on a more poignant significance.

Kate thanked the concierge for his help and turned away from the desk. After working for a few hours, she'd changed and come down to ask for directions to a good restaurant. The tall, gray-bearded Belgian couldn't have been more obliging, loading her with tourist information and a map of the city on which he'd circled several possibilities.

Crossing the hotel lobby, she gripped the map between her teeth, trying to push the stack of leaflets into her already bulging purse. Suddenly she collided hard against someone wearing a very familiar white sweater. The leaflets and map went skittering across the white marble floor.

Kate reeled back from the impact, looking up to see Myles Hunter's surprised face as he reached out to steady her. His touch sent a tingling shock through her shoulders, bared by the thinly strapped bodice of her violet cotton dress. Hastily she stepped away, almost tripping over herself in the need to detach his hands from her skin. To hide her flustered embarrassment, she knelt and began picking up the scattered brochures.

"Are you all right?" He crouched down beside her and helped gather the last of the papers. A quick upward glance brought her face-to-face with his faintly puzzled expression.

Pulling herself together, she smiled, careful to keep her inner turmoil from showing. She couldn't let him see how easily he affected her.

"Fine . . . I'm sorry, I wasn't looking where I was going. It was my fault entirely." She stood up, finding it difficult to hold those shrewd gray eyes as he rose with her. She needed to escape. "Well . . . see you later."

His gaze flicked to the jacket on her arm and he moved to block her exit. "You're going out?"

"Yes. I'm going to have some dinner and get in a little sightseeing. I know I'll be too busy for it tomorrow."

"You're going out alone?"

The tone in his voice, implying he felt entitled to an answer, annoyed her. "Quite alone."

"Well, I'm sorry, but I can't let you do that." His manner was that of a man used to giving orders and having them obeyed.

"What?" Kate gasped. Had she just heard right? "Why ever not?"

"Because it isn't safe," Myles said slowly, as if he were speaking to a child.

"That's ridiculous," she laughed, "I'm quite capable of looking after myself. Thanks anyway, but you don't need to be concerned."

"Yes I do, and I repeat, I can't let you go out alone."

Of all the nerve! Bridling at his presumption, Kate said shortly, "Excuse me," and moved to step around him, when his hand shot out, gripping her arm.

She tried to pull away, but his fingers tightened relentlessly, just above her elbow. People walked back and forth in the busy lobby, not paying any attention to them. What if she yelled, made a scene? She glared at him in impotent anger, trying hard to wrench her arm from his grasp. Suddenly, to her horror, she felt her throat tighten, and tears of frustration began clouding her vision. Fighting hard to keep them from spilling over, she hardly trusted herself to speak.

"Let go of me right now," she said through clenched teeth.

His face blurred, his fingers slackened, but still he didn't release her. Gently but firmly, he led her out of the lobby and into the nearly deserted lounge. Hailing a passing waiter and ordering two dry sherries, he took her over to a quiet table.

"Sit down," he commanded, finally letting go of her arm.

"Who the hell do you think you are?" She wanted to slap his arrogant face and go stalking out of the room. Only the thought of it all ending up on the front page of tomorrow's paper stopped her.

With an ill grace she ignored his order and glared at him resentfully across the small, round table. "You have no right to treat me like this." Her voice quivered as she fought hard for control. "I'm not a twelve-year-old . . ."

"Then stop behaving like one," he said curtly. "Sit down and listen to me."

"Look." She remained standing. "Ever since our first meeting, you've made it quite obvious you don't like me . . ." He opened his mouth to speak, but now that the floodgates had been opened, she wouldn't be sidetracked from her determination to set him straight. "But for reasons of your own you agreed to have me along. i'm here to do a job, just like you are. I'm also an adult, and quite capable of taking care of myself. Now, I would appreciate it if you'd stop treating me like an irritating nuisance and ordering me around at your whim like some flunkey!"

"Are you quite finished?" he asked, maddeningly cool and controlled.

"No, I'm not. You can also remember to keep your hands to yourself. Perhaps you enjoy pushing women around. But I'm not . . ." Kate stopped, shooting a mutinous look at Myles, when the waiter appeared at her elbow.

The tall, balding man looked from one to the other as his customers stood glaring at each other across the small table. With an eloquent Gallic shrug, plainly implying that all *les Anglais* were mad, he set down the drinks and left.

Kate sat down abruptly, and after a second so did Myles. With angry defiance she picked up the glass and tossed back a large gulp. The liquid burned a path down her throat, making her grimace and shudder at the taste. She hated sherry.

Suddenly, Myles grinned and Kate couldn't tear her eyes away from his face. It was extraordinary the way the smile transformed him. It was the first spontaneous emotion she'd seen from him, besides hostility. Kate looked down and fidgeted with her glass. Without her anger to shield her, she was beginning to feel awkward and self-conscious, and took another sip without meaning to.

"Don't keep drinking it," his amused voice ordered. "I'll get you something else."

"Don't bother." Quickly she set down the glass, irked by his patronizing tone. "Do you think you can manipulate women that easily? Just smile, and they'll melt into a little puddle at your feet?"

He looked down into his glass, an amused half-smile hovering on his lips. "What a hazard that would be to good Italian leather . . ."

Kate blinked. Had he just made a joke?

"Look," he continued. "I'm sorry I was a bit high-handed about it, but it really is dangerous for a woman to be out alone at night. Brussels isn't exactly one of the safest cities in Europe, and you're a stranger here . . . As part of the tour, I feel responsible for you."

Astonished even further by the apology, she slumped back into her chair and stared open-mouthed at him. This about-face from overbearing autocrat to concerned big brother left her completely disoriented. What was he up to? Was this just another act he was putting on for her benefit? Well, this time she wouldn't fall for it so easily.

He must have seen her suspicion. "Come on, Kate, you have to learn to trust people sometimes."

She blushed at the deliberate mimicry of her outburst in his library. Since when did she blush? Looking up, she saw his mouth was unsmiling but his eyes held an unmistakable gleam of mocking laughter.

Even though she distrusted his motives, she couldn't help responding to this unexpected provocative mood. He dazzled her, made her feel completely out of her depth. Her heart knocked against her ribs alarmingly, a warm flush spreading under her skin. It must be the aftereffects of the sherry. It had to be.

She gazed mesmerized, noticing the fine lines raying out from his eyes. Warm gray-blue now, they held hers, calm and unwavering, with no clue to what was going through his mind. The alcohol must have gone to her head, because right now she wanted more than anything to reach across the little table and ruffle her hand through his silky blond hair.

The stronger, saner side of her knew she should get the hell away from him before she acted like even more of a fool. But the other side of her wanted to stay right there and hope to move him to another, less fleeting smile.

"Well, thank you for explaining this to me." She avoided his eyes. "I have to confess, I never thought it might be dangerous. I'm so used to doing things alone. I lived in New York for two years, you know." Her tone implied that nothing more needed saying. "I can take care of myself."

"I'm quite sure you can," Myles said with a patronizing smile. "Nevertheless, I *do* feel personally responsible."

Kate tensed at his tone. "That may be," she stood her ground, "but you have no right to dictate to me. I don't work for you, and even if I did, this is my time off. I'm going out. If you feel so responsible, then you can come to dinner with me and play bodyguard."

That characteristic eyebrow rose skyward as Myles made a visible effort to grapple with his astonishment and Kate wondered in amazement where those words came from. She hadn't intended to say that at all.

After a moment's hesitation he spoke. "All right. I'll just go and change. I'll be back in a few minutes." He stood up and walked out of the lounge.

Kate's jaw fell open in stunned disbelief. Had he just agreed to go out to dinner with her? And since when did she invite internationally famous people to be *her* bodyguard?

But as her stupefaction wore off, it occurred to her that whatever the reason, this was a valuable opportunity to learn more about him. Even if none of it ended up in the article, she had an urge to try to make sense of all his contradictions, find out what lay behind the facade.

When they first met, he had seemed completely impenetrable, but she'd already begun to pick up on small idiosyncrasies that betrayed the emotions he tried to hide. Like the way he raised one eyebrow when he was disconcerted.

A stream of well-dressed people flowed in throu'' the open doors of the lounge for drinks before and Kate noticed Tony among them. With a s a smile she attracted his attention.

He hurried across the lounge to her table into the opposite chair. "I've been looking How about a bite to eat? I can highly recomm dining room, the Michelin guide gives it three s

"I'd love to, but I've made plans with Myles." Kate faltered slightly over the words. They sounded so glib, as if going out on a date with Myles Hunter were an everyday occurrence. *Hang on a minute, stupid. This is not a date.*

Tony looked surprised. "I'm glad to hear it. Does this mean you two have buried the hatchet?" Obviously their antagonism hadn't been lost on him.

"Yeah . . . in my skull." Kate laughed and went on to tell him briefly what had happened, while Tony sat looking thoughtful.

"Heaven knows what prompted him to agree. Considering the way he's treated me up to now, I'm amazed . . . By the way," Kate went on tentatively, "I couldn't help noticing at the press conference last week and today on the radio, he came across very pleasant and relaxed. I had the impression he thought all media people were the scourge of the earth."

Tony gave a wry chuckle. "Well, actually he does. But he also knows he has to play the game to be successful." He leaned back in the red swivel chair and slowly rotated it back and forth. "He distrusts the media. He's done his best to avoid them for a while. But it's necessary for this tour, so now dealing with them is part of his job."

"So he can turn the charm on and off when necessary," Kate said cynically, thinking of their little episode earlier on. Naturally she hadn't mentioned to Tony the disturbing effect Myles had on her senses.

"Isn't that true of most people? Especially performers whose lives are so exposed."

Kate tugged at her bottom lip pensively. "He may charm the rest of the press, but I can't help noticing that around me he doesn't bother putting on a front."

"I don't think you know him well enough to make that assumption." Now what did Tony mean by that? "And he did let you come along. Granted, the record company and I encouraged him to cooperate, but if he'd vetoed the story that would have been it."

Kate mulled this over in silence. So much for assuming he'd been pressured into it. She was beginning to realize that no one pressured Myles Hunter into anything.

"You know, if you think about it, it's one thing to be faced with a press conference and quite another to have someone dogging your steps, knowing your slightest offhand remark can be taken out of context and end up in print. Just imagine not having a private life, Kate."

"I *have* imagined it. I don't think I could do this job without wondering what it's like to be on the other side. You know there *are* limits to what I'll do to get a story." Somehow it was important that Tony believed her. "I know he doesn't trust me, but I don't want to intrude on Myles's personal life. That's not the kind of story I'm here to write. Do you think he'll ever agree to the interview?''

Tony leaned forward, his brown eyes narrowing with keen penetration. ''Don't give up hope just yet. You've got three weeks. My advice is to tread carefully, respect his privacy, and he'll let you know when he's ready. And don't ever forget . . .'' he emphasized, ''he works very hard at all of this, and he insists on controlling all aspects of his career. Myles expects a lot from the people who work under him and he doesn't suffer fools gladly. There may be times when the best thing to do is stay out of the way.''

His warning might be well-intentioned, but it had come too late for her.

''So . . . he likes to pull all the strings,'' Kate murmured.

Tony laughed at her doubtful expression. ''He's not that hard to get along with, ask anybody who's worked with him.''

She smiled wryly. ''Unless you're a reporter.'' She met the humor in Tony's warm brown eyes and laughed softly. More and more she found herself liking Tony. She could be so relaxed and comfortable with him, unlike Myles who made her feel like she was walking on eggshells all the time.

She glanced up and stiffened, seeing the man who filled her thoughts silhouetted in the doorway. She felt her heartbeat quickening as his gaze found their table, resting on her for a second, then sliding over to Tony.

He walked into the room with a graceful stride, hands in the trouser pockets of his elegantly loose-fitting black suit. Kate wasn't the only one watching his progress. Heads turned in recognition, and the background buzz of voices increased a notch or two.

Too sophisticated to besiege him for autographs, this crowd wasn't so blasé as to ignore him, either. The women especially. Expensive coiffures were pushed away from perfectly made-up faces. She watched them discreetly craning their necks for a better look as he walked by, oblivious to their scrutiny.

His physical beauty was undeniable. Not just in his lean, striking face. It was apparent in the way his body moved, fluid and smooth. In the way he radiated sexual magnetism.

Kate shivered. This man was dangerous. A woman would be better off tied to the tracks of an oncoming train than involved with someone like him. He wouldn't be the kind of man you'd ever get over. Or the kind who would stay. He'd break a heart without a second thought, and remain untouched. All these things she sensed just watching him. Never, ever could she let her thoughts stray in that direction, she told herself as he reached their table.

THREE

Why? That was all he could ask himself as he paused in the doorway and scanned the dimly lit room. Kate still sat where he had left her, but now Tony had joined her and they were deep in conversation. Damn it, they were already acting like old friends, but whenever he was around she behaved like a cat on hot bricks.

Why did he care? For that matter, why was he going out to dinner with her? And why hadn't he sent her packing for her refusal to do as she was told? But then again, why did it concern him if she wandered the dangerous streets alone?

The tears . . . they were his undoing. Who would have expected her to succumb to tears after all he'd put her through already? A thick-skinned reporter should be able to put up with anything. But she surprised him, and not many people did that anymore.

Well, if she had to come along, it might be amusing to try to discover just what Miss Kate O'Brien was made of.

He took a chair from a nearby table and pulled it up to theirs. A waiter approached with discreet speed, but he waved him away.

Myles looked at her, his gray eyes speculative. "Are you ready to go now?"

"Umm . . . Yes," she said hesitantly, dazed at how swiftly their relationship had changed. Half an hour ago they were fighting, now they were going out to dinner.

"Want to come along, Tony?" he asked. "After dinner I thought I'd show Kate around. She wants to go sightseeing." His mocking tone made her feel like a hopeless tourist.

"No thanks, I've seen Brussels. One old European building is pretty much like the next one to me. Besides, I've got a stack of paperwork waiting for me upstairs." He shuddered. "I'll just have a quick bite and get to it."

Myles shook his head. "You're a complete philistine, Tony." He turned to Kate. "He doesn't even like museums. Incredible, isn't it?" There was that glimmer of amusement again.

Tony snorted and rolled his eyes. "Museums! God help me, Myles, you've dragged me through more boring musty corridors than I care to recall. I've done my duty. Give me the twentieth century any day." He pushed back his chair and stood up.

Kate rose from the table feeling awkward and uncertain. She walked out of the lounge at Tony's side, acutely aware of Myles just a half step behind her. Tony told her he would drive her to the stadium in the morning.

"I'll call you when I'm leaving then." Saying good night, he walked off toward the elevators.

Kate turned toward Myles uncertainly, desperately groping for something to say to break the awkward silence, but he broke it first.

"This must be your lucky day."

"Why?" Could he be so incredibly conceited that he was referring to the honor of his company?

He glanced at his watch. "It's just past nine; the museums are all closed."

His expression gave nothing away. It took Kate a few seconds to realize he was being facetious. She smiled quietly.

"Actually, I quite like museums." Maybe he did have a sense of humor after all. An answering smile lurked at the corner of his mouth.

"Fortunately not all the interesting sights close their doors early. Shall we go?"

His hand lightly touched her bare back, where the deep V of her dress left her skin exposed, sending a shiver down her spine. As he guided her across the dim splendor of the lobby, her heart began to speed up. If she was dreaming she didn't want to be awakened.

"Just one thing, Kate . . ." He paused and dropped his hand, suddenly looking blank and somber. "From now on it's off the record, right?"

That brought her down to earth.

"Of course," she nodded automatically, her voice dull. She felt like an idiot. Their whole relationship of journalist and subject had been briefly obliterated by her purely feminine response to him. Not for a second could she afford to forget it again.

Pulling on her jacket and slinging her bag over her shoulder, she moved slightly away from him. She still couldn't get over Myles agreeing to go out with her, but maybe he might be actively trying to put their relationship on a more comfortable footing.

Perhaps this was an ideal way to get more relaxed with each other. And perhaps if she had a better sense of him as a mere mortal, it would help her shake this juvenile reaction he kept inspiring in her. They went through the heavy glass revolving doors that took them out of the hotel, and into the evening streets of Brussels.

Although still overcast, it was a pleasantly warm evening in early June, the soft breeze full of the promise of summer. The sun was setting somewhere behind the clouds, the dull-gray sky becoming darker by the minute.

Myles quickly led Kate away from the broad, busy avenue, into the old section of town. Down into the narrow side streets crammed with little shops and restaurants where no cars intruded. Lamps on the building walls shed pools of yellow light in the shadowy lanes.

Kate had never seen so many restaurants so close together. On both sides almost every second doorway led into a dim interior jammed with little tables spilling out into the street, all filled with laughing, talking people. Delicious aromas floated by, reminding Kate how hungry she felt.

"Charming, isn't it?" Myles asked her as she peered into a shop window filled with exquisite examples of fine-cut crystal and Belgian lace.

"This is exactly the type of scene I always imagined as Old Europe." Kate knew she sounded like a typical tourist. "You know, I've never been to the Continent before. That's one of the reasons I wanted to do this story."

"Aha . . . so now I know two reasons. Are there any others I should know about?"

The casual little smile he directed at her sent a tingle up her spine, making every little hair on the back of her neck stand up. Had he guessed that her interest was more than just journalistic? She knew this was ridiculous, but he made her feel paranoid and guilty, as if he could read every thought going through her head.

Her smile felt stiff and awkward. No matter how hard she tried to be casual, the evening still felt unreal. If she didn't start behaving normally he'd guess the effect he had on her and there was no way on earth she could continue with this assignment if that happened.

"Of course, you could have chosen a more leisurely

way to see Europe. A music tour is worse than one of those bus trips. You know . . . if it's Tuesday, this must be Belgium.''

Kate laughed, relieved that he hadn't noticed her discomfort. ''Well, it's only Monday, and I'll just have to squeeze in as much as I can along the way. Of course, this is all old hat for you, I suppose. You seem to know the place quite well.''

That was an understatement. Myles had really surprised her with his knowledge of Belgium; its people and their history. As they walked he continued pointing out the landmarks of the city, seeming to know something about all the major buildings they passed and the collections housed in the now-closed museums.

''And there's St. Michael's Cathedral,'' he told her, pointing up at the massive building, its gray bulk looming in the twilight, dominating the hill above them.

''It's a lovely example of Brabantine Gothic.'' Kate stared up at the ornately decorated pinnacles and turrets, the complicated stone tracery. ''But I'm afraid it reminds me too much of a birthday cake,'' she concluded with a laugh.

''You really *do* know something about architecture,'' Myles said with a surprised, appreciative smile.

''Just a little bit . . .'' Kate confessed. ''But I read about the cathedral in the guide book back at the hotel. I just wanted to sound knowledgeable,'' she grinned, and he laughed quietly. ''And I have a little confession to make about that book you were reading on the plane.''

''Yes, I thought you would. Your research department must be quite clever.''

''Oh, no. That's not it at all.'' She shook her head. ''I would never pretend an interest just to impress someone. That would be dishonest.'' His step faltered and he shot her a quizzical look as she continued. ''The truth is, my brother is studying architecture, and he sent me that book. I must say, though, I'm amazed at how much you know about this city and its buildings.''

He shrugged it off. ''There's no point in traveling if you don't find out something about the places you go to; it keeps it amusing.''

But he was just too well informed to explain it away as idle curiosity. Knowing how little formal education he'd had, it gave her a new respect for his intelligence and the seriousness of his interest.

All at once, Kate realized the awkwardness between them had vanished. She was behaving more naturally and Myles had loosened up, becoming more talkative and entertaining. God, how he intrigued her. It would be very easy to fall under his spell completely. At that moment he looked down at her with a heart-stopping smile.

''Are you hungry?''

''Starved,'' Kate replied with feeling.

''Good. There's a little place right over there I've been to before.'' Myles pointed to a low, timbered doorway, set in the stuccoed wall beneath a dimly lit sign inscribed Waeyten's Raadskelder. ''Do you like seafood?''

Kate nodded, completely charmed at this point, knowing her journalistic detachment was suffering badly. Following the sweetly nostalgic sound of an accordion, they walked down narrow stone steps into a dark, low-ceilinged room, lit only by the candles on each of the little round tables.

From their table tucked into a corner, she listened to the soft murmur of intimate conversation, couples lost in each other in the charmed circle of candlelight. If there was ever a more romantic setting she had never seen it. Without stretching her imagination too far she half expected to see strapping young hussars straight from *The Student Prince* seducing beautiful young peasant girls.

With a start, she came back to reality as an elderly waiter arrived at their table. She'd have to get a grip on this absurd romanticism.

"*Deux sole Meunières*," Myles ordered, then looked over the wine list. Kate stared at him, torn between bemusement and irritation. Did he always order for other people without consulting them or did he just do it with her? Why didn't she say something, instead of sitting there like a spineless wimp, letting him take charge.

He leaned back in his chair and crossed his arms, eyeing her with that cool, speculative look she was beginning to know so well. Kate fortified herself with a deep, steadying breath. If he was trying to intimidate her, he'd have to try a lot harder. The wine arrived and she took a sip from her glass, holding his gaze without flinching.

"What made you choose journalism?"

Kate blinked, then stared in confusion. She had been gearing herself up for something inflammatory, or provocative at the very least, but the seemingly harmless question threw her off her stride, especially when he added, "You don't strike me as being ruthless enough for the job. You're too vulnerable."

"I . . . I'm tougher than I look," she said faintly. "Believe me, I had to learn the hard way."

"Yes, I imagine you did. You're an attractive woman. Depending on your attitude, that could be an advantage or a disadvantage in your profession. I'm sure you've had your fair share of come-ons, although some reporters I've known treat them as one of the perks of the job."

"I've always thought of it as one of the nuisances. Although I'm better at handling them than when I first started out."

Was she still making sense, or had the shock of hearing Myles Hunter call her attractive deprived her of

coherence? *That's right, Kate, keep on babbling.*
Maybe he won't notice that you're delirious. And all
because he made some offhand comment.

"I'll never forget my first interview. It was with Richie Raven."

Myles raised his eyes and groaned.

"Do you know him?" she asked.

"Yes, I've tripped over him occasionally. What was
the name of his last album . . . *Scum of the Earth*?
Highly autobiographical, wouldn't you say?"

Kate choked on the sip of wine she'd just taken and
started to laugh. "That was *Son of the Earth*."

"If the shoe fits . . ." He shrugged and smiled. "So,
tell me what happened."

"What happened was, I got stalked around a room
by this oversexed, egotistical reptile passing himself off
as a musician." He raised his eyebrow and she almost
laughed, knowing he had got the point, but some devil
spurred her on to needle him some more. "He claimed
he'd mistaken me for a groupie. I finally had to set him
straight with a knee to the groin."

Myles groaned and briefly shut his eyes. "I guess I
got off lightly. Had I known how ferocious you were
I would probably have thought twice about my little
pretense."

"The point is," she shook her finger at him, "with
Richie Raven I didn't get that interview . . . but since
then I've learned to handle myself in any situation."
Kate sat back and crossed her legs, sending him a challenge with her eyes.

"Okay, Kate, you can stop being so subtle. I get the
point." Myles sent her a sizzling look through narrowed eyes and laughed, a low, throaty chuckle that
held a note of appreciation. "I admit you handled yourself very well, but . . . any situation?" He leaned forward with a capricious smile that in anyone else would
have suggested mischief.

"I'm here, aren't I?" She lifted her chin in a deliberately cocky gesture.

Damn, but she was good. Her argumentativeness drove him crazy, but on the other hand, he couldn't resist the challenge of that self-possessed defiance. He knew he'd been guilty of deliberately provoking her into these verbal fencing matches, not so much to win a point, but because the sparring made him feel stimulated and alive.

And she enjoyed it, too. Looking at her across the table, he could tell by the glow in those beautiful sea-green eyes, the flush in her cheeks. By the way she used her small, fine-boned hands when she was trying to make a point.

Her contradictions had him intrigued. That guileless, offhand comment about honesty had taken him aback. She really seemed to mean it. How could someone that ingenuous end up in a business that almost demanded duplicity?

"You just don't seem cutthroat enough for this job, Kate. You've got the guts, I'll grant you that, but are you prepared to lie through your teeth and run rough-shod over people's lives in pursuit of the almighty story?"

She shifted in her seat, feeling defensive. Yes, lots of reporters *were* like that, but it irked her that he couldn't see her as an individual. "You don't have to be insensitive and aggressive to be a good reporter, you know."

"Really? I've never encountered any other kind, until now." His quiet reply effectively took the wind out of her sails. "Or perhaps you're more subtle about it, the velvet-glove treatment."

So, he was still suspicious of her. "That implies the iron fist underneath . . . and I don't need to be that devious." Why had she let her defenses down and become so relaxed with him?

His eyes slowly slid over her. "Yes, I can see that . . . I think you could get what you want in other ways." His voice was insinuating, his gaze like a physical caress.

Kate felt her cheeks beginning to burn. Was he deliberately doing this because he'd sensed her reaction to him? Was he trying to trick her into making a fool of herself? Or did he just enjoy exercising his power over women?

"I've always been honest and straightforward in my job. That's what works best for me."

In one prim gesture she sat back, crossing her arms stiffly in front of her. Suddenly her thin jersey dress seemed absurdly inadequate. His gaze made her feel naked. In the intimate isolation of the candle glow he was looking at her with a warmly seductive, promising look. The way she dreamed he'd look at her in her girlish fantasies. Did he even know he was doing it?

He took her reply in silence, picking up the coffee spoon and playing with it absently. Kate found her gaze drawn once more to those slender fingers. Not wanting to face his disconcerting eyes, that unguessable look. Not wanting to know what lay behind it.

"Then that must be the secret of your success."

Her startled gaze flew up to meet his eyes but could detect no sign of sarcasm. "Thank you," she murmured uncertainly.

"You see, Kate, I've done *my* homework too." He crossed his arms on the table and leaned toward her. "I make it my business to know something about the people around me, and I've learned a great deal about you."

She felt a quiver of uneasiness at the thought of being investigated and examined. For the first time she had a true inkling of what it must be like for Myles, who had to live his entire life under public scrutiny.

While she was still reeling from his first revelation he hit her with another one.

"I've been reading a few of your articles. They're good, although I could do without your attempts at psychoanalysis." He paused and laughed at her expression. She didn't know whether to be pleased or affronted. "Come on, Kate. It's only rock 'n' roll, right?"

"I should think you, of all people, would appreciate an attempt to get beyond the usual trivial gossip and say something meaningful." She lifted her chin a little higher and felt the tell tale burning of her cheeks.

Good answer, Kate. Could you get a little more pompous next time? Perhaps she had gotten a little pretentious in that last series of profiles she'd written in New York. He probably thought her an insufferable pseudointellectual.

"Do you always investigate the people who work with you?"

"Why are you so surprised? If I'm going to let someone come along on the tour and poke their nose into everything, I want to know what to expect. I'm not some brainless wonder who lets the manager look after it all," he told her calmly.

Kate stared, at a loss for words. On the one hand she felt insulted to be characterized as a prying snoop. Then on the other hand . . . he was looking at her in a way that made her feel anything but insulted.

Her eyes met his, alive with amusement. But with something more intimate in their smoky depths, a warmth she'd never seen there before, she could feel it spreading through her. Mesmerized, she knew this prolonged eye contact was dangerous but couldn't tear her gaze away.

"Monsieur . . . Mam'selle . . ." The waiter arrived, to Kate's profound relief, placing before them generously filled plates. Taking an immediate intense interest in her food, she assumed a careful nonchalance.

"Gosh, I'm so hungry!" she said inanely. *For God's sake, pull yourself together*, her inner voice commanded.

"Tell me, Kate, do I rate so low in your estimation that you think I'm incapable of simple common sense?" His eyes had never left her face, the corners of his mouth curving with a hint of amusement.

"Far from it. It's just that, to be honest, I'm surprised you liked my work. But you know . . ." she went on frankly, "I have a feeling I'd be wise to expect the unexpected from you."

He laughed, low and husky. Such an intimate, attractive laugh, it made her pulse speed up.

"Yeah, I like that. Expect the unexpected." He laughed again, then looked at her thoughtfully for a moment. "If it's any consolation, you were rather unexpected, too." While Kate wondered what he meant, he continued. "I'm not an easy person to work with, Kate; remember that. I hope you make it all the way through."

The ominous note behind his cryptic statement only added to the confusion inside her head.

Talk about mixed signals. First of all he hadn't wanted her there, he'd been cold and arrogant. Now he was being friendly . . . not merely friendly, but turning on her the full force of that sex appeal that had millions of women the world over fantasizing about him. And now this warning. How could you ever know where you stood with a man like him?

"Don't worry," Kate replied airily to hide her confusion, "I'm tougher than I look."

"Good," he smiled, looking down as they both began to eat.

"Do you like your dinner?" he asked after a while, when they had nearly finished. Kate nodded silently, her mouth full of food. "I'm glad. I hope you didn't mind my ordering for you?" he asked with a sly smile.

Kate swallowed and shot back swiftly, "You hope nothing of the sort. You wanted to see if I'd tell you where to stuff your sole Meunière. You wanted to see if you could irritate me, knowing I have to stay in your good graces if I want this story. Well, Myles, I'm giving you fair warning . . ." She leaned forward, challenging him. "I *want* this story, and I usually get what I want."

Myles stared back at her with dawning appreciation, and laughed. Damn it. Why did she have to get more attractive all the time?

"You caught me," he admitted, raising his wineglass in salute. "You *are* full of surprises."

Kate couldn't help but smile, gripped by heady exhilaration as if champagne were bubbling through her veins. Did Myles feel it, too? Was that the reason his eyes shimmered with sensual awareness, intense and exciting?

After the plates were cleared and the coffee ordered, he suddenly asked, "Tell me, is there a *Mr.* O'Brien?"

Kate stopped short for a moment at the unexpectedness of his question. Myles smiled down at the tablecloth, tracing the damask flowers with his spoon, his tone too carefully casual.

"I thought you'd done your homework," she said evasively. He looked up and met her eyes and she found herself answering honestly. "No . . . no, there isn't."

"I find that hard to believe."

"Why?"

"Come on, Kate, I didn't think you were the type to fish for compliments."

"You keep talking about my type. I hate being categorized."

"Really? But that's exactly what you and your colleagues have done to me. Painted me as some kind of Casanova.''

Kate felt a twinge of guilt. This time she couldn't be self-righteous. She might not have swallowed the worst stories, but she'd certainly assumed he wasn't a monk.

''If I'd had half the women you've credited me with, I'd be dead from exhaustion by now.''

Silence reigned for a long uncomfortable moment.

''I'm still wondering why you're unattached. Tell me, is there no love interest on the horizon?'' Myles persisted, carefully studying his wineglass, running his finger around the rim with concentration.

''No.'' Kate felt strangely compelled to answer.

''You're not even a little in love?''

''Not even a little in lust,'' she tossed off flippantly, as he looked up directly into her eyes, pinning her with his gaze.

''Are you quite sure?'' he asked, point-blank, and she knew with complete certainty he had read the truth all too plainly.

''Look!'' Abruptly she went on the attack. ''How did we get to be talking about me? I'm supposed to be interviewing *you*.''

''What's the matter, Kate, don't you want to talk about it? Some deep-seated psychological fear of intimacy?'' he mocked.

It was exactly the type of conclusion she might jump to, the type of manipulative questioning she herself had used to get a response, and he knew it. Being on the other side was incredibly galling. Putting himself in control of any situation apparently came very easily to Myles.

''What, no response from the hotshot reporter? What's the matter, Kate? Don't you have anything brilliant to say?''

Only the laughter beneath his words took away their

sting. With a grudging smile she shook her head. How could she be really angry when he was so dead-on?

"Round one to Myles Hunter." She chalked up an imaginary score.

"You still haven't answered my question." He took a sip of his wine and smiled at her knowingly.

"No, I haven't."

"Well?"

"No comment."

For a long silent moment his eyes held hers, awareness vibrating between them so strongly, Kate almost expected the candle to begin madly flickering.

This had to stop right now. The coffee arrived and she slowly sipped it, steaming hot and bitter. No possibility of harmless flirtation existed here; the atmosphere between them was too inflammable.

Did he deliberately manipulate the situation to show his power, his need for control? How typical she must seem, falling for that calculated blend of arrogant charm and sexual magnetism. Her inability to resist his allure infuriated her.

Myles motioned to the waiter for the bill, then glanced down at his watch. She sensed his mood change with dazzling swiftness.

"It's late. We'd better get back to the hotel." Now the shutters were back on his eyes as he looked up, the impassive mask back in place.

It was as if another Myles had briefly emerged, then just as quickly retreated back into the protective shell. For a while she'd been feeling as if they were on the same level. Then, with a glance, he'd put her back in her place, reelevated himself.

As they left in silence, Kate walked up the steps, feeling intensely confused and disoriented, as awkward as on that first meeting. No, it was worse. He had found the chink in her armor. If she had felt vulnerable before, she felt completely exposed now.

Myles, you're playing with fire. And being a hypocrite to boot. Her pretended toughness would probably vanish and she'd run a mile if she could see the seduction scene that had been playing through his mind. Somewhere along the line the amusing game of provoking her had got out of hand.

He'd begun to find it very difficult to avoid imagining what lay beneath that tantalizing scrap of violet cotton and had barely been able to keep his eyes away from the tempting suggestion of hardened nipples straining against the thin fabric. For one reckless moment he had wanted to reach out and touch, run his hands along the smooth curve of her shoulders, discover if her skin was as satiny soft as it looked.

But he couldn't afford to let himself think about her this way. Besides, he never mixed business with pleasure and, honest as she might be, she was still a member of the press. They'd tried to destroy him once, it would be madness to give them more ammunition. A dalliance might be tempting, but not at the price of seeing his private life dragged through the muck all over again. Cool and distant, that's how he would play it from now on.

Winding through the narrow streets, Kate glanced up at him occasionally, seeing him abstracted in thought. Apparently he'd forgotten her presence completely. So much for all that fascinated interest in the restaurant. Well, what did she expect from someone like him, she told herself scornfully. Being the object of adulation must breed an ego that saw other people as rather insignificant.

It was after midnight, and much quieter now. Fewer people strolled the warren of little streets. Thank goodness Myles knew his way around; she'd completely lost her sense of direction.

Without warning, they emerged from the narrow lane into a huge open space, a square enclosed on all sides by massive Gothic buildings, the narrow streets leading into it invisibly. Kate gasped in amazement, wandering toward the center, in awe at the overwhelming grandeur.

Rain had fallen while they were in the restaurant. The cobblestones shone damply and a fine mist hung in the air. It was happening again. That persistent effect Europe had on her, like stepping back in time. They were completely alone, the silence broken only by their quiet footsteps. Forgetting Myles's presence, Kate couldn't contain her enchantment.

"This is wonderful," she whispered excitedly. "I feel like I've strayed into a medieval fairy tale . . ." The silence was dreamlike, the statues in their niches looking as if they might step into life at any second. "It's like *Sleeping Beauty*, where everyone is waiting for the Prince to break the spell . . ."

Suddenly she caught herself. What was she saying? He must think her a juvenile idiot, prattling on naively about fairy tales. She turned her back in embarrassment and heard him laugh quietly.

"It has that effect on me, too . . . except I always see it filled with gallant men on horseback, ready to ride off and brave Napoleon on the field of Waterloo . . ." Turning slowly to face him, she saw he was gazing at the buildings, his eyes unfocused and far away, his voice low. "All those hopeful young faces, expecting glory and finding only death."

At his words a vivid picture sprang into her mind, her throat tightening with emotion. The panic, the suffering, the women and children left behind to mourn. Unexpected tears clouded her vision. She looked up to catch Myles watching her, then he smiled sadly. That smile reached in and captured her heart. They had just shared something very intimate and special.

With a sigh, he shook his head, his manner becoming more brisk. "This square is called the Grand Place," he said, and began telling her about the buildings hung with colorful medieval banners, limp now in the damp stillness. It was fascinating, yet, as she listened, part of her mind still lingered on that intimate moment of a few minutes before.

In that magical moment they had touched something real in each other. He had let down his guard. It made her feel privileged and strangely protective.

She could use this in her story. It would be a wonderful, personal insight. But she couldn't betray the implicit trust she'd briefly felt between them. Besides, he'd made the city come alive for her, and for that she'd always be grateful.

She turned impulsively. "Myles . . . thank you so much for bringing me here. You've given me a wonderful memory to take home." Her smile faded as she met his eyes. He was closer than she expected. All the powerful sensual desire that had been simmering just below the surface all evening could be ignored no longer.

His slow gaze dropped to her mouth, then back to her eyes again. She melted to the spot, hypnotized, like a moth hovering over a flame. Unaware she'd been holding her breath, she let it out on a resigned sigh, just as he lowered his mouth to hers. All that baiting, all that circling, had been leading up to this inevitable moment.

Their lips met and they moved together as one, passion flaring instantly, like setting a flame to a gas jet. His tongue seduced her willing lips to part and explored her mouth with a deep, searching intensity, sending shock waves of desire racing through her.

She felt his hands burning a path down her bare back with unbearable eroticism. When his firm palm moved to cup the swelling curve of her breast beneath the soft fabric, he shuddered and pulled her closer, his fingers stroking the betraying tautness of her nipple.

Mindlessly she arched against him, trembling as his tongue continued its inflaming exploration. Even in her forbidden imaginings, it had never felt so wonderful. Almost swept away in the flood of overpowering sensation, her will suddenly reasserted itself.

No! This was getting completely out of hand. She was losing control of everything. It was all wrong. With all her strength Kate pushed him and he reeled back in shock, taken by surprise. They stood looking at each other, breathing fast and shallow.

Still trembling with aroused need, Kate felt aghast at the shattering intensity of that kiss, at the shaming response of her body. For an instant Myles looked astonished. Then, in the blink of an eye, the mask was back on, he was cool and distant.

Quivering with resentment and terrified that he had sensed the depth of her attraction, Kate lashed out defensively, ''What kind of game do you think you're playing? Was that another little test?''

"Get things in perspective Kate. It was only a kiss," he taunted, calm and unmoved.

"Yes . . . and a very unwelcome one!"

"Really? You felt very welcoming a minute ago." He sounded positively smug.

Kate bit down on her lower lip, still throbbing and swollen from the caress of his mouth, her cheeks burning with shame. "How dare you say that! You can bet your life it won't be repeated," She tried in vain to ignore the way her bare skin still tingled with the imprint of his hands.

"Not unless I want it to be."

His insolent expression made her feel like screaming; she could barely maintain a seething restraint.

"Your conceit knows no bounds, does it? You're so used to women making fools of themselves over you." Her heart still pounded frantically against her ribs. "Well, I'm not going to be one of them. And if you think you can make me turn tail and run home without the story you can think again. That's exactly what this carefully orchestrated little evening was supposed to achieve, wasn't it? Well, it's not going to work!'' she finished breathlessly, grabbing up her bag and jacket from where they had fallen, hands shaking with repressed fury.

A brief flicker of surprise crossed his face, quickly vanishing, replaced by that same cool, ironic smile. Turning on her heel, she stormed off. From behind her back came his amused voice as she headed toward the shadowy opening of the nearest side street.

''Knowing your talent for directions, are you quite sure you know how to get back to the hotel?'' His words held mocking laughter. Kate stopped dead in impotent frustration. So much for her grand exit. She had absolutely no idea which way to go.

FOUR

Myles stepped into the shower stall and ruthlessly turned the tap fully on. He gasped at the blast of icy spray on his heated flesh.

Cool and distant. What a bloody joke. He'd been cool and distant for all of ten seconds. One glance at that softly quivering mouth of hers had sent logic right out the window. He swore savagely and stuck his head under the freezing torrent.

Damn it, the woman was attractive, but not *that* breathtakingly beautiful. There'd been plenty of beautiful women in the past ten years and he'd never had any trouble resisting their charms if it proved inconvenient. And it hadn't been convenient nearly as many times as they'd credited him with.

He wrenched off the tap, picked up a thick white towel off the rail and rubbed himself dry, noticing with a wry grimace that the cold shower was highly over-rated as an antidote to rampant lust.

What the hell had that woman done to him? He slipped on his terry bathrobe, strode into the bedroom of his suite, and flung himself down on the billowing duvet to glare up at the ceiling.

Damn her . . . and her fairytale fantasies. Discovering a full-blown romantic hiding under that feisty exterior had disarmed him so much he'd let the circumstances get the better of him.

Come on, Myles. Stop kidding yourself. Ever since the first time you saw her you've wanted to kiss her. Okay . . . so he'd kissed her. Now that he'd satisfied his curiosity he'd better leave it at that. How fortunate she had even given him a convenient way out, accusing him of trying to scare her off. If he was smart he'd take it.

He groaned wearily and got to his feet, turning down the duvet and shrugging off the bathrobe. He caught sight of himself in the dresser mirror and smiled wryly. Every one of his thirty-six years showed on his face tonight. Years spent learning the necessity of keeping pain at a distance. That had been one lesson he'd salvaged from the hell of his life with Alison.

From her perch high above the side of the stage, Kate's gaze wandered over row upon row of empty seats filling the huge stadium. Tonight they would be packed with eager fans, all there to see one man. The man who had filled her thoughts all morning as she prowled the stadium taking notes and photographs, anxiously preoccupied with the prospect of facing him again.

The camera dropped in her lap as she leaned back, laced her hands behind her head, and sighed, looking up at the clouds dotting the blue sky above. Right now their evening together, the kiss they had shared, seemed like a dream.

What did a kiss mean to someone like him? A casual amusement, nothing more. That seductive intensity was just practiced expertise. But for her . . . ? A smile curved her lips at the memory.

All morning she'd resisted thinking about it. Finally

she gave in and closed her eyes, reliving the kiss in exquisite detail. His delicious taste, the faint scent of his aftershave, the silky feel of his hair between her fingers, the fiery conflagration inside her when his tongue invaded the depths of her mouth.

And those long, sensitive fingers moving over her skin, driving her mad with unfulfilled desire. At merely the thought she felt her nipples tightening, straining against her tank top until even the slightest friction of the soft cotton was almost unbearable, making her ache for his touch once more. Her back arched in involuntary supplication, a soft moan escaped her lips, and a little shiver of desire trembled through her.

''Penny for your thoughts.''

The husky voice behind her shocked her back to reality. She jerked upright, feeling her face burning.

Myles stood a few steps above her in the aisle, his tall, lean frame encased in loose, pleated tan pants and safari shirt, sleeves rolled back in the warmth of late morning. He wore a slouch hat pushed back on his head, the sun shining on the blond hair showing beneath the brim.

How long had he been standing there watching the play of emotions cross her face? As he walked down a few steps to her level she stood up, fumbled in her pocket for her sunglasses, and slipped them on. If she were going to stay professional and pretend nothing had happened last night, she'd need something to hide behind.

''You surprised me, Mr. Hunter.''

''You called me Myles last night.'' Why did he have to bring that up? ''There's no need to be formal anymore. By the way, I hope you enjoyed our little . . . exploration.'' Was he deliberately trying to increase her discomfort with that lazy smile?

''It was fascinating.'' Some perverse instinct made her reply with bored sarcasm. She felt even more grateful for the dark glasses now, but they couldn't hide the flush in her cheeks.

"Did you sleep well? I know Tony hauled you down here pretty early." The amusement flickering in his eyes made her feel absolutely transparent.

"Slept like a log," she lied.

He stepped closer and pulled off her sunglasses, slipping them into his breast pocket.

"Give me those." She went to snatch them back, but he covered his pocket with his hand.

"I like to see people's eyes when I talk to them. It forces them to be honest."

"I thought you didn't believe reporters capable of honesty."

"I don't."

He sat down in the aisle seat, effectively blocking her exit. Reluctantly, she took her seat beside him. He turned toward her, leaning his bare, muscular forearm along the top of the seat, his lean fingers almost grazing the tip of her shoulder. She shifted uncomfortably, edging away a little, acutely aware of his steady gaze. Turning her attention down toward the handkerchief-size stage, she could see the swarming crew members rolling on the speakers.

"I was just watching the setup," she lied, anxious to steer the conversation into safer channels. "It's so much more complicated than I ever realized."

"Not unlike people, wouldn't you say, Kate?"

She turned her head and met his gaze boldly. If he refused to be deflected, she might as well take the bull by the horns. "Certainly when it comes to you. You're one of the most complicated people I've ever met."

"Really? I thought you had me pegged as a manipulative, dictatorial egomaniac who likes to push women around. Do you suspect there might be further undiscovered depths to my obnoxiousness?"

She couldn't suppress a chuckle. "If I find anything else I'll let you know."

"I'm sure you will."

His droll inflection made her smile broaden. Those gray eyes turned warm and smiled back and suddenly she could feel it happening all over again. Except this time she couldn't blame it on the romance of candlelight and a deserted square. Even more reason to adopt a more professional attitude. She looked away, aware that his intent gaze hadn't left her face.

"I'd like to meet some of the crew and get their perspective on all this." Kate waved a hand toward the hive of activity below.

"Good idea, you can be sure of getting a different point of view." Suddenly he was allowing her to change the subject. "In fact, why don't I introduce you to a few people."

As she thanked him in surprise for the unexpected offer, Myles rose to his feet. Kate stepped out beside him and they began walking down the steep aisle.

The heel of her sandal caught on a step and she stumbled. Blindly, she reached toward Myles for support at the same time as his strong arm encircled her waist, pulling her up against him. Her breast yielded to his hard chest, and she tried to ignore the tantalizing pressure of the edge of his hip against her stomach. She looked up to thank him and the words died in her throat. Deep in those silvery eyes a turbulent intensity flared, then just as quickly vanished.

Making sure she'd regained her balance, he let her go and moved away to continue down the steps in silence.

Kate gave him a sideways glance to see his face once more an impassive mask. Was it a glimpse of blazing passion she had surprised in those cool, gray eyes? She sighed. Myles looked over at her; she met his expressionless gaze squarely. Now what? Once more his mercurial mood changes left her disoriented.

They walked down the seemingly never-ending steps until they were on the field, behind the stage set at one end of the huge oval stadium. The high barriers extending from each side formed a protected area of grassy field where the tents and trailers housing the musicians and crew were scattered.

Two bare-chested roadies in cut-offs were rolling a large cumbersome road case up the ramp onto the stage, others were onstage setting up the drums and keyboards. In the open scaffolding beneath the stage a technician sat at a desk fixing cables. Everyone looked busy and purposeful, unlikely to welcome idle chitchat.

Kate turned to Myles, startled to find him right behind her. Fighting back a sense of panic, she turned away again, breathlessly conscious of the heat of his body almost touching her own.

"This doesn't look like a good time for introductions," she croaked, then nervously cleared her throat.

"It won't get any better."

His warm breath fanned the nape of her neck, making the fine hairs stand on end. She shivered involuntarily. Anxious to put a little distance between them, she stepped forward, but he followed and placed a firm hand on her back, propelling her toward the stairs leading up to the back of the stage.

"Come on, I want to introduce you to Andy, my production manager." He took her up the steps and as they crossed the open stage Kate noticed the curious glances.

"Hey, everybody," Myles stopped and took her elbow, pulling her closer. "I want you to meet Kate O'Brien, from *MusicBeat*. She's on the tour to do an article. If you look pretty for her, you might get your picture taken."

The crew had all paused and were treating her to an assortment of grins, smiles, and stares, but Kate barely registered any of this. Myles's warm hand had slid casually up to her shoulder to rest on her bare skin, his lean fingers absently tracing the edge of her tank top, causing her heartbeat to gyrate wildly.

She didn't dare look up at him, afraid of what her face might reveal, or had the tremors racing through her body already given her away?

"There's Andy." He pointed toward the wings where a burly man in grubby shorts and a worn T-shirt stood screaming at some poor roadie. "On second thought, why don't we catch him when he's in a better mood." He chuckled deep in his throat and turned toward Kate.

She swallowed hard and said the first thing that came into her head: "I get the impression he'd be a demanding man to work for." She knew how inane that sounded, but it couldn't be helped. She needed time to recover her poise. If only he wouldn't touch her, then she'd be able to cope.

"He's a bastard, but he's no worse than me," Myles grinned.

Maybe if he wouldn't smile. That was it, no touching and no smiling, *then* she could cope.

"It's no picnic setting up this complicated show in different cities. You only get one shot and it has to be perfect every time. Andy's one of the best, that's why he works for me." Myles had been talking as they walked back down the steps, but she'd barely caught half of what he said. She had to stop this nonsense and get a grip on herself.

With a profound sense of relief, she saw Tony emerging from the catering tent. "If you want a ride to the hotel, I'm leaving now," he called out as he walked toward them.

"I'll be right there." She jumped at the opportunity to escape from Myles's disturbing presence. Besides, she needed to write up the morning's notes and change out of her shorts into something dressier for the concert.

Myles walked them to the car and held the door open for her as Tony got in and started the engine.

"Thanks for showing me around and introducing me; it was more than I expected." Kate pulled together the tattered remnants of her spirit and returned his steady gaze.

"I don't want you to think me uncooperative." With a devilish smile he pulled her glasses out of his pocket and placed them in her hand. "You can have these back now, but you won't need them with Tony."

He was right, because with Tony she had nothing to hide. But Kate slipped them on anyway, and got in.

Myles closed the door and they drove away. Immediately she felt the tension ease from her body. Around Myles she could never feel comfortable. Fight or flight, those seemed her only choices. Well . . . she wasn't about to run away.

"That's not good enough. It has to be perfect. Do you understand? Perfect."

Kate and Tony got out of the car to the sound of Myles's angry voice over the PA. A moment later he came striding off stage and walked purposefully over to Andy, who'd been waving a walkie-talkie and yelling at the soundman when they drove in.

"I'll be waiting in my dressing room until you have this sorted out. Don't keep me waiting too long." Fists balled with tension, he pushed his hands into his pockets and started walking away.

"It's okay, Myles, we're working on it," the production manager called after him. "Don't worry, it's under control."

No wonder tough, forbidding Andy Sprye sounded like he was soothing an angry tiger. She remembered that steely tone of voice only too well.

Kate smiled nervously at Myles as he approached,

but he just gave her a preoccupied nod and turned to Tony.

"Why did this have to happen on opening night? I hope this isn't an omen of things to come."

"Come on, relax. Everything will be fine, you know it will." Tony turned to Kate. "Why don't you go over and introduce yourself to the band. I'll catch up with you before the show."

As she watched Myles walk away with Tony toward his trailer, she fought the urge to run after him. Clearly he was worried. After three years without performing, a lot of money and a lot of credibility were riding on this tour. The desire to comfort him and ease his anxiety was so strong it took her by surprise.

Not that he'd want her around witnessing his insecurity. He'd probably throw her out on her ear for being in the way. And besides, it really had nothing to do with her. She'd better just stick to her job.

The musicians' dressing room turned out to be a large tent. Half of it was curtained off for privacy, the other half a makeshift lounge, furnished with a battered old red velvet couch and chairs and a couple of tables. Only two of the four musicians were there, playing darts, when Kate entered.

"Hi, hope I'm not disturbing you." She paused, holding the tent flap open.

"You can disturb me anytime." Kate recognized Steve, the tall, blond drummer. "Wanna play?" He held out the feathered shafts with a smirk that told her he wasn't just referring to the game.

"Thanks," she accepted. She'd got his number. It would be a pleasure taking Mr. California to the cleaners.

She introduced herself while taking careful aim at the dartboard hanging on an upturned road case. "So guys . . . how does it feel to be back on the road with Myles again?"

Bull's-eye.

"That was a lucky shot, beautiful," Steve whispered behind her.

Kate ignored his hot breath against her ear and followed it up with two more swift bull's-eyes, retrieved the darts, then slapped them down hard into his palm.

By her third win in a row Steve had stopped swaggering and begun treating her more seriously. He and Paul, the small, dark bass player, insisted on a rematch.

"This girl's a shark," Paul complained.

She laughed at his ludicrous expression. It helped to have a dad who was champion of the local Darts League.

Steve's eyes suddenly flicked over to the tent opening behind her. "Hi, Myles."

Kate turned to see him stop on the threshold, fixing her with a morose gaze before he walked into the room and flung himself down on the sofa. She turned back to the game with a sigh, but out of the corner of her eye she saw Myles stretch his legs out in front of him, watching the dart game with a hostile frown.

Could it be plain and simple stagefright making him so edgy? He was always so confident and controlled, that possibility hadn't occurred to her until now. But then she thought of a show-biz veteran she'd interviewed who'd confessed to spending the last thirty years being violently sick before every performance.

Despite Myles's moody presence on the couch, she squeaked a win in the last game and Steve and Paul quit in disgust and went off to the courtesy tent for dinner.

She flopped down beside Myles, who turned and looked at her impassively.

"I know you're worried, but Tony's absolutely right . . . everything will be fine. I saw every concert you gave in Toronto, and I was never disappointed."

A halfhearted smile crossed his face. "Ah . . . a diehard fan. Have I just discovered another reason why you wanted to do this story?'' His smile broadened and he turned slightly toward her, folding his arms across his chest.

''It's no good. You're not going to goad me into an argument this time.'' She smiled at him. ''I'm determined to remain understanding and supportive.''

He was grinning now. ''Oh . . . is that what you're doing? Well, I suppose I should be grateful.''

''Don't strain yourself.'' Her dry inflection made him laugh. ''Hey, how about a little music to help you relax.'' She jumped up and reached for the portable tape player on the table by the couch.

Myles stopped her with a hand on her arm. ''No music. I need to think about my own music before I go on. Why don't you just come and sit down beside me and talk to me some more.'' He patted the faded red cushion beside him and smiled up at her.

She sank down next to him, filled with a warm glow of happiness. He made her feel that she was helping him in some way.

For the next half hour they sat and talked about the most inconsequential things, and Kate sensed his tension gradually ebbing.

''Hey . . . where is everybody?''

She looked up, startled to see Tony poking his head through the tent opening.

''We're back on track, Myles. I'll go round up the rest.'' He disappeared, and Kate realized she'd almost forgotten about the bustle and tension of the backstage world outside. She got up to put the darts away in their case, lying open on the table by the couch. As Myles walked past her toward the door he gently brushed her cheek with one finger. When she looked up he winked and smiled before following Tony out the door.

For the rest of the afternoon Kate floated around backstage in a happy daze.

Just before the show she poked her head around Myles's dressing-room door to wish him luck. He nodded abstractedly. He looked a little pale, she thought, but composed.

Kate took the lens cap off her Nikon. Amid the rising noise from out front, she stepped around the barricade into the six feet of no man's land in front of the stage. She froze for a split second. From the steel crowd barrier in front of her to the farthest reaches of the vast stadium she could see nothing but people, a seething, roaring, many-headed monster. No matter how often she stood here, the experience always filled her with awe and made her nerves tingle with apprehension.

Already hot, it felt even more sweltering now, near the mass of tightly packed bodies. Thankfully, it had clouded over. The sun was almost down, the concert timed to begin just after sunset.

Powerful lights flooded the field as the sky darkened. Ragged cheers broke out every time a figure walked on stage, then died away when it proved to be just a crew member doing a last-minute adjustment. No matter how many concerts she covered, Kate always buzzed with the rising excitement. As the minutes ticked by, the suspense was becoming unbearable.

Everything went dark, the crowd hushed in the last glimmering threads of twilight. And then a disembodied voice boomed out. "Ladies and Gentleman . . . Myles Hunter!"

With a crash the music began, white lights illuminating the clear, graceful columns framing the stage, the band, in darkness. A single spot picked out the lone figure standing near the back and the audience went wild.

Myles bounded stage front and launched into a burning, passionate version of "Dance with Me," one of his biggest hits.

On the other side of the barrier frenzy reigned.

Screaming, crying girls tried to fling themselves across the six feet that separated them and take him up on the invitation. The security men busily pushed them back down. with the show barely underway they had their hands full already.

It quieted down a little as the mood became gentler, the songs slower. Kate took picture after picture. He looked incredible. She could think of no other word for it. Lit to perfection, his pale suit reflecting the colors of the superbly coordinated lighting, this was another Myles entirely.

Kate stood looking up at him, forgetting to take pictures for a moment. Her heart leapt inside her, pounding erratically, feeling churned up and emotional, overpowered by longing. Smiling into the crowd, warm and intimate, he was weaving a magic spell over the whole huge audience. Holding them in the palm of his hand, caressing them with his voice.

The crowd surged in response to every gesture, like a woman responding to a lover's touch, a willing partner in seduction.

Every nerve tingling in the sexually charged atmosphere, Kate's hips swayed fluidly with the music, until she felt drugged with desire. Suddenly she became aware she was unconsciously emulating Myles's movements on stage, her body in harmony with his rhythm.

It was all too much. The uncontrollable frenzy of the masses behind her had become too frightening. She had to get away.

She scrambled to the safety of the wings. The desperation receded as she perched on a stool behind the monitor board and looked out at the audience, into the sea of faces, all those girls screaming and crying. How could they give him that kind of power, make themselves so vulnerable?

How much of what she felt could be attributed to the

teenage crush she'd had for an unattainable idol, and how much was real?

Then he sang the song which had become her favorite. The same dreamily sensual love song she had heard yesterday on the radio. Watching him pour his heart out, she forgot to tell herself it was an act, forgot about the thousands of adoring women out there in the darkness, forgot about everything but that haunting emotional voice that seemed to sing to her alone.

He turned and looked straight at her for a moment as their eyes met. " 'You'd never need to doubt my love for you . . .' " If Myles Hunter had sung to her at seventeen, she would have been reduced to a little puddle on the side of the stage. Who was she kidding? Even now she felt her knees weakening. Did she have that same vacuous look as those teenage girls out in the audience?

But it was different now. She had glimpsed the other Myles. The man behind the mask. The man she felt a consuming desire to know more deeply. A cold shudder of fear raced through her, the same fear that had clutched her at twelve years old, the day she went skating on the lake and fell through the ice. She'd never forget the paralyzing terror that clutched her when she couldn't touch bottom in the dark, icy water. Was she skating on thin ice? Was this a premonition she should turn tail and run?

All too soon it was over, the encore finished. Myles dashed off stage to a deafening roar, and Kate slumped in exhaustion, emotionally wrung out by the experience.

The hospitality tent abounded with the usual bizarre mixture of characters. Kate could barely push her way in and get a soft drink from the bar; she didn't feel like battling the crush over to the food table. Business-suited record executives, temporary passes stuck on their lapels, lavished attention on the beautiful women in designer labels who posed carefully for any stray photographer. They made her feel suddenly dowdy and underdressed in her simple denim mini and plain white shirt.

Myles had been half listening to the record company PR man, his eyes scanning the crowded tent, until he found her. He watched Kate make her way over to the bar and get a drink. Just the way she walked, the graceful sway of her hips, pleased him.

He liked the natural way she met people's eyes and smiled, she looked so relaxed. And he liked her style, the clothes she wore. His eyes followed the length of her slender legs from the white leather sandals all the way up to the firm, molded curves so tantalizingly outlined by that little blue skirt. What was she wearing under that oversize shirt? He remembered only too well the feel of those small, firm breasts cresting with desire under his palms.

Kate took a sip of her Pepsi, turned, and suddenly saw Myles through the crowd. She caught her breath. He was staring at her, his aristocratic features expressionless. But his eyes watched her with a dark intensity she found disturbing. He seemed uncaring of the fawning people celebrating around him.

But his band were lapping it up, each surrounded by a little knot of girls. Steve pushed past her on his way out, his arm around a tall, smug blonde. He seemed to have the rest of the night all planned.

"Miss O'Brien! . . . *MusicBeat*, right?" A short bespectacled man beamed up at her excitedly as Kate tried to decide if she knew him.

"Arnie Finklestein." He grabbed her hand and pumped it furiously, a superfluous gesture seeing they were pressed intimately together already by the crowd.

"Ragtop Records, A and R. Remember me now?"

How could she forget the ubiquitous artist and repertoire man. Arnie seemed to pop up all over the place promoting one dreadful band after another.

Today, however, he might have his uses. Kate asked how the sales of Myles's new album were going and he responded so enthusiastically, her pen could barely keep up with his mouth.

Myles smiled to himself at the sight of Kate patiently listening to Arnie and nodding her head occasionally. He didn't envy her. Once the little weasel smelled free publicity he was like a terrier with a bone.

She'd been so sweet this afternoon. Everyone else knew enough to leave him alone when he was in that dangerous mood, but she had gone charging in where even Tony dare not tread. Would she still have done it if she'd been warned? He looked at her, smiling at Arnie and scribbling madly in that little book of hers. Yes, she'd still do it. She didn't scare easily.

He felt a tug on his arm and smiled mechanically down at the heavily made-up face of the aspiring new singer who'd just been signed to Ragtop Records.

As a promotional gimmick the record company wanted him to pose with her to help give her career a push. He wished to God it was all over. He'd felt so good tonight, playing for an audience after so long. Somehow seeing Kate standing in the wings singing along with his music had given him unexpected pleasure.

Looking over Arnie's balding head, Kate paused for a second and her pen stopped moving. Through the crowd she saw Myles engrossed with a tall, stunning brunette. Cameras flashed as she clung to one arm, ruffled his hair, and planted a kiss on his cheek. Myles smiled down at her intimately.

Why didn't she just take off her clothes and make love to him right here? Feeling bitchy and irritated Kate turned away. The statuesque beauty made her feel miserably plain and unattractive. How could she ever have seriously believed Myles could desire her, when he had women like that throwing themselves at his feet?

No wonder he'd been so nice to her today. He felt

sorry for her. He saw her as an object of pity for naively misinterpreting his arch games as real sexual interest. *That's right, go ahead, let this man turn you into a complete neurotic!*

"Miss O'Brien . . . Miss O'Brien . . ." Arnie called after her in vain as she pushed her way blindly through the crowd. "I haven't finished yet."

"Well, I have," she muttered to herself.

Tony suddenly appeared at her side. "Are you going now, Kate?" he asked in surprise.

Steve pushed past them on his way back in, alone now, obviously looking around for another conquest. She felt sick. Men like him summed up the whole rotten business. For a while she'd almost allowed Myles to convince her he might be different.

"Yes," she answered briefly.

"Let me give you a ride back to the hotel," Tony offered.

Kate didn't even bother trying to mask her cynicism. "Surely you don't want to leave all the fun and excitement?"

He shook his head. "This life in the fast lane isn't my speed, I'm afraid."

He looked around the crowded room, and Kate sensed he was just as much of a misfit in this scene as herself. He put an arm around her shoulder to steer her through the crowd. At the entrance, she looked back to see Myles watching them leave, his expression unreadable.

What was wrong with her? Ever since meeting Myles Hunter she'd been on an emotional roller coaster; depressed, jealous, angry, infatuated . . . When would it ever end? It was so unlike her normal calm, reasonable self.

She's leaving with Tony. So what? She was free to do whatever she wanted. But she hadn't even bothered to come over and see him. *That's all right. It doesn't matter.* But it did. And now he wished he could tell all these bloodsuckers to go to the devil so he could leave.

Kate sighed as she lay back in the scented water and willed herself to relax . . . This wasn't working. Tired but restless, a bath had seemed the ideal way to wind down after she got back to her hotel room. It should have been blissful.

Preserved from modernization, the huge old bathroom with marble fixtures and massive claw-footed tub remained a sybarite's retreat, complete with fluffy towels, luxurious bath oil, and scented soap. Kate smoothed the lather slowly over her legs in lingering, preoccupied circles.

All she could think about was Myles. His voice . . . his eyes . . . his hands . . . what he must be doing with that damn brunette right now. Try as she might, she couldn't stop tormenting herself, imagining them entwined in passionate lovemaking.

Her body arched restlessly. She wanted him, it was pointless to keep denying it. Her swollen breasts ached with longing for his touch, wondering what pleasures making love with him could hold. She hadn't the faintest right to feel jealous, and it was insane to let herself think about him this way.

She pulled out the plug and got out of the tub, feeling frustrated, angry, and much too wound up to sleep. Wrapping herself in the fluffy hotel bathrobe, she phoned room service and ordered a pot of tea . . . a large pot. It was going to be a very long night.

FIVE

At the very top of the stands in Dusseldörf Stadium,
Kate stood beside Myles on the wide, canopied deck,
looking down over the tiers of seats falling away below
them. The crew down on stage were setting out the
huge trusses with their attached assemblies of swiveling
varilights. Soon they would winch the massive con-
struction high above the stage.

It was a familiar scene now. As familiar as the
clutching crowds, the spine-tingling roar of approval
when Myles took up the microphone. After the triumphant opening in Brussels, five days in Scandinavia had
taken them through Copenhagen, Stockholm, and Hel-
sinki, and now down into Germany.

Kate leaned her elbows on the railing and sneaked a
sideways look at Myles. That little scene in the square
might never have happened. Why, she felt almost relaxed with him now. No . . . relaxed wasn't exactly
the word, because he never lost that sense of reserve,
and she would sometimes catch herself feeling the bizarre unreality of being this close to someone she'd
once idolized. She still felt a little quiver every time

she saw him, but now she could congratulate herself on ignoring it quite successfully.

His little game hadn't scared her off, and if it had been some kind of test, she must have passed. He had clearly resigned himself to being pleasant, and now that he had relaxed a little, too, she liked what she saw.

Kate stepped back from the railing and took the lens cap off her Nikon with the sudden impulse to capture this unstudied moment.

Myles glanced toward her. "Haven't you taken enough pictures?"

"This one's just for me. For my album." She stepped back and looked through the viewfinder, focusing carefully as he turned and leaned back against the railing. His plain white shirt was open at the throat, exposing a triangle of tanned golden skin. Loosely pleated tan trousers accentuated his lean hips and long legs. He had more natural style than any man had a right to.

"Surely you can pick one you've already taken."

Kate shook her head. "You don't understand. I want a picture of the real you. Not the facade you present to the public."

"Okay, Sigmund Freud, here's the real me." He leaned back against the railing and crossed his arms.

The real Myles? She must have seen that pose a hundred times. The one she always thought of as his patented *GQ* look. Kate lowered the camera.

"That's not what I want at all. You could at least take off your Ray-Bans."

He took them off. His gray eyes wore a lazily sensual smile that made her knees feel slightly weak. Oh, God, did he even know he was doing that? Or was it an intrinsic part of him? Maybe it would be better if he put them back on.

"You still don't get it," she sighed. Letting her camera drop to swing loosely against her white tour T-shirt, she put her hands on her hips. "Will the real Myles Hunter please stand up?"

He frowned. "I don't understand what you mean."

Kate stepped closer. "Don't give me one of your standard, careful poses. I've seen them all. I've photographed them all! I want to see the real you. Show me some honest emotion."

A flash of devilish inspiration seized her. Suddenly she reached for his face. He leaned away, puzzled, but she pulled him toward her and kissed him full on the mouth. His body went rigid.

She stepped back, raised the camera, and snapped the shutter. She laughed at his expression, a mixture of bemusement and outrage.

"Thanks. That's exactly what I wanted." Still laughing, she started to turn away. His hand shot out and grabbed her arm so that she almost fell into him. Reaching out to steady herself, her hands pressed against his chest. He gathered her close, trapping her against him, and before she had time to react, his mouth came down on her parted lips.

At the touch of his lips on hers, her body caught fire, the moist seduction of his tongue entwining with hers fanning the flames until she feared they would consume her. She molded herself to him, sliding her hands up around his neck, twining her fingers eagerly in the thick silk of his hair.

He shuddered and wrapped his strong arms around her so tightly she could barely breathe as his mouth savaged her lips, then left a trail of moist, burning kisses down her neck to the little hollow at the base of her throat.

Her small moans of pleasure vibrated against his lips and the smell of her perfume was driving him to the brink of madness. He wanted it all, he didn't know what he wanted next. In an agony of desire he sought her lips again, desperate to taste her sweetness, to feel her softness, and to submit to the heady torment of her tongue entwining with his.

His kiss slowed, became less hard, as his mouth moved searchingly over hers and she returned the caress with uninhibited eagerness, knowing she was arousing him, too.

Suddenly he drew away from her. She slowly opened her eyes, bereft at his unexpected desertion, to find him watching her closely, his expression unfathomable.

"Why did you do that?" she asked.

He gently pushed her away and crossed his arms in an oddly protective gesture. "Why did you kiss me?"

"I wanted to get a reaction," Kate said more steadily, beginning to collect herself.

"Well, you got one, didn't you? When you go around trying to provoke reactions with methods like that, you might get more than you bargained for."

"I didn't think I had to worry about that with you." The cool, analytical tone of their conversation astonished her, yet the slight betraying flush on his cheekbones made her think he wasn't as unmoved as he'd have her believe.

"Why? I'm a man. I have all the normal male responses."

"I never doubted that for a moment. I just didn't think you saw me in that way . . ." She trailed off, embarrassed in case he thought she was fishing.

Kate began walking down the long, steep flight of stairs. Myles said nothing as he fell into step beside her.

He couldn't do it. He couldn't go on fighting the attraction. Just the feel of her soft, fragrant body in his arms, her passionate response to his kiss, for those brief moments he wanted her so badly he could have made love to her right then and there.

He hated being out of control. It made him feel vulnerable and fragile. Feeling that way always led to pain, and he'd had enough pain. Better to be comfortably numb.

There was only one way to solve this problem, although mixing business with pleasure might not be wise. On the other hand, they both wanted each other and there was only one rational solution. As long as she didn't have expectations he couldn't fulfill. He heard her sigh and turned to look into her troubled green eyes. What would she think if she knew what he had in mind?

Kate sneaked a look at Myles. He was frowning down at the steps, deep in thought. Feeling the tension in the air, she laughed nervously.

"Don't worry, I won't try to provoke any more reactions from you."

"I think it may be too late for that," he said quietly.

He stopped and she looked up at him. His face bore an enigmatic look, a taut smile she couldn't fathom, but it sent shivers through her. Had he guessed her secret? Guessed at all those emotions she had so carefully buried since leaving Brussels. She had been kidding herself they could just be casual acquaintances.

"It's pretty warm up here. Would you like a cold drink?" He looked at her as if expecting her to refuse.

"Yes. Thank you." Her awkward acceptance didn't seem to give him any pleasure. The paradox confused her. Did he want her company or not? Continuing down the steps, they made their way backstage to the motor home that served as Myles's mobile dressing room.

Behind the privacy fence surrounding it stood a white table and chairs, shaded from the hot sun overhead by a large green-and-white striped umbrella. Myles installed her there, then disappeared into the nearby courtesy tent, coming back a minute later with two glasses.

"This time I thought I'd play it safe and get you something nonalcoholic . . . I wouldn't want to make the same mistake twice.'' He handed her the tall, icy glass of lemonade with an amused look in his eye.

''Thank you . . . You're absolutely right, I do prefer this,'' she laughed, thinking what a picture she must have looked choking down that sherry like disgusting medicine.

Myles responded to her amusement with a small, intimate smile, sending a quiver through her. There was a warm light of appreciation in his eyes. Kate felt bewildered. As soon as she thought she had a grip on his mood, it changed.

''So . . .'' He surveyed her over the brim of his glass. ''Tell me . . . what else don't you like?'' His low, intimate voice held a caressing quality that made it virtually impossible to stay cool.

''I don't like being reminded of embarrassing moments,'' Kate replied as Myles smiled back, silently saluting her with his glass. ''And besides, haven't we got this the wrong way around again? Aren't I supposed to be the one asking the questions?''

She began feeling breathless, self-conscious. His gray eyes held hers for a moment, then traveled slowly down to her mouth. She could almost feel his lips touching hers again.

''What do you want to know?'' he asked, his voice caressing as he slowly raised his eyes back to meet hers. His look scorched her. The air between them sizzled with sultry awareness.

Instinctively she sensed there were depths to his passion she didn't know how to deal with. He touched something deep inside her, making all her previous experiences seem shallow and frivolous. She knew that all too well from the helpless, fervent response he drew from her.

''I want to know who you are.'' The slowly measured words came out of their own accord, surprising her.

"You don't ask much, do you?" Sardonic amusement lurked in the glittering depths of his narrowed eyes. "Well, you can try and find out, but you won't be getting any help from me."

"Frankly, I didn't expect any."

"It might be interesting to see what you can find out. Of course," he added with an almost conspiratorial smile, "It's well known how closely I guard my secrets."

"Everyone has their secrets."

"Including you, Kate?" He raised an inquiring eyebrow.

His soft, velvety tone sent a warning shiver up her spine. Getting involved with him would be like playing with fire. Besides, she didn't even know if she was reading him right. She knew from experience he could turn this seductive act on and off.

He leaned a little closer. "Well . . . you try to find out about my secrets and I'll try to find out about yours."

"There's nothing very interesting to find out."

"Let me be the judge."

No, she wasn't mistaken. The subtle warmth of his inflection sent a clear message. But it left her confused. What did she want? Had she subconsciously tried to provoke this response when she kissed him?

"There you are!"

Tony's face appeared around the fence and he cheerfully joined them at the table, completely oblivious to the awareness crackling between them. Kate looked down into her glass, trying to pull herself together, then glanced at Myles, her heart pounding hard.

He coolly greeted Tony, as if all the implied sexual undertones in their conversation had never been there. Clearly he was nowhere near as affected by the mood. Or perhaps, once again, she'd read too much into it.

"How was London? Did you get those contracts sorted?" Myles asked.

"You're booked into Hammersmith for two nights instead of Wembley."

"Great. I've always liked the old Odeon; it's smaller, more intimate." He glanced at Kate.

"I knew you'd feel that way." Tony sat back in his chair and smiled.

What if Tony hadn't interrupted them . . . was this how it started? That journey to his bed?

Suddenly Kate realized she had begun to really like Myles Hunter . . . and not just because of the wanton lust he inspired in her. He was a captivating mixture of contradictions: intelligent, perceptive, but also moody and unpredictable. Her fascinated response to him had begun to scare her.

Tony filled Myles in on his crowded schedule of meetings, interviews, and TV appearances. Meanwhile, Kate sat distracted, stricken by the thought that she wanted Myles to care about her, the way she was beginning to care about him. She felt shaken and a little desperate with the need to get away and mull it over by herself.

"I'm going to get some lunch." Kate jumped to her feet abruptly.

Tony looked up, startled by her sudden movement, but in Myles's clear gray gaze she saw accusation, and she knew that he thought her cowardly. But what disturbed her more was the hint of regret.

"So how many brothers do you have?" Tony asked with a grin as Kate took a bite of her smoked salmon on toast. "With a name like O'Brien, I imagine a big Irish family."

"Only half Irish," she explained. " . . . And not that big. My dad came from Dublin and met my mom in Canada. Besides myself there's Sean, Patrick, and Maggie.''

Fate just wasn't on her side. Tony had blithely spiked her getaway attempt by telling her that lunch for three would be served at any moment. At least he was there to be a buffer, although if it weren't for him she'd be safely away from Myles's brooding presence.

As the luncheon progressed, Tony got her talking about her Irish cousins and told her about his own family, but Myles stayed conspicuously silent.

"You know, Tony. I'm surprised you aren't married," Kate said. "I could imagine you surrounded by your own raucous brood of kids." She noticed Myles's mouth tightening in disapproval. Had she mentioned a taboo subject? But Tony didn't seem to take offense.

He smiled pensively. "If it was up to me, I would be. I was married, but it didn't work out."

"I'm sorry," Kate murmured. "I didn't mean to pry."

She couldn't look at Myles. She just knew he must be glaring disapproval. She was probably confirming his stereotype of the nosy reporter.

"That's all right. It doesn't bother me to talk about it. I wanted kids, she didn't." He shrugged. "Things just fell apart . . . How about you, Kate? I'm surprised someone with looks like yours hasn't been snapped up by now."

"No," Myles interposed. "I have it on good authority that our Kate hasn't yet been tempted to take that trip down the bridal path." It was the first time he had spoken.

Kate grimaced. "Who would you suggest I take it with, Richie Raven?" She spat out the words. "The only men I meet in my job are musicians. They're unreliable and promiscuous and the worst risk in the world."

"My, my . . . aren't we cynical." Myles raised an

eyebrow. He exasperated her. How dare he play this cat-and-mouse game?

Returning to the empty courtesy tent at five, Kate sat down at a table and loaded her camera with fresh film, then scribbled a few additional notes. Over the PA she could hear the soundcheck; the monotonous, methodical setting of sound levels for the drums, guitars, and keyboards. Hearing Myles's voice, she decided to watch him do his vocal check.

She walked around to side stage. He looked so comfortable, so natural, in front of a microphone, unintimidated by the huge, empty field, by the prospect of the thousands who would fill it tonight.

They launched into a song, then Myles glanced over, saw her standing in the wings, and waved down the band. As the music petered out, he called to her.

"Come here." He held out his hand and smiled his encouragement.

Confused and suspicious, she held back. He shot her a devilish look, then turned to the band.

"Let's do 'Tonight.' " As they began playing the slow melody, he walked over and took her hand, drawing her out to the middle of the stage where he began singing to her. Kate felt her cheeks burning.

" 'Come into temptation' . . ." he sang. " 'Lose yourself with me.' " After everything that had happened that morning it was a virtual invitation into his bed. The crew was standing around watching, the band was grinning at her discomfort. Everyone was laughing at her, laughing at the reporter being put on the spot. But it would have been so much worse if they knew how serious he was when he offered,

" 'Can't we be lovers, tonight
I still believe in you and me, tonight'."

Underneath the mortification of being publicly propositioned lurked a secret delight Kate didn't want to acknowledge. He wanted her, and he was telling her in such a romantic way. The song ended and he stepped away from the microphone, still holding her hand. Very quietly, so no one else could hear, he spoke.

"How about it Kate . . . tonight?" There was a trace of impatience in his voice as he tugged at her hand. "Come, come . . . let's stop the games. Don't keep me in suspense."

Disappointment formed a painful lump in her throat. He thought she was a pushover, she could see it in his eyes, hear it in his voice. What a fool she'd been, thinking him so romantic.

He'd just played his trump card, that was all. Seducing her with his voice, making her feel the song was for her. But wasn't that his secret? Every woman who listened to him thought he sang for her alone. Kate pulled her hand away, furious. How many others had fallen for it?

"For someone who says he hasn't known that many women, you certainly have a slick line. But you'll have to try harder than that." She saw the surprise in his eyes at her disparaging tone. "Perhaps you should try this trick on one of your fans tonight. I'm sure you'll meet with instant success."

Turning away with her head held high, Kate strode off into the wings, her body stiff with anger. She ran down the steps and made it as far as the courtesy tent before Myles caught up with her, grabbed her arm, and swung her around.

"Don't try to tell me you're not interested." His clipped tones made her anger come to the boil.

"And don't try to sell me on your inexperience, okay?" She wrenched her arm out of his grasp and stormed into the empty tent.

Myles followed. "Come on, Kate." His jaw tightened

with impatience. "Let's stop these silly little games and act like sophisticated adults."

"Am I supposed to throw myself into your arms now? You certainly have a romantic way of wooing a woman." She turned an insolent back to him and poured herself a cup of coffee, her hand surprisingly steady considering her fury.

"I think we both know what we want. Why wrap it up in meaningless rituals?"

She turned to face him. "Meaningless rituals? Speak for yourself. *I* still have boring provincial values. I can't casually jump into bed with just anyone." She looked at him contemptuously for a second, then walked away and put her coffee on a table, preparing to sit down. He spun her around and gripped her shoulders, his fingers digging painfully into her flesh beneath the thin cotton shirt.

"Then why did you kiss me this morning?" he demanded. "You can't deny the desire that's always there between us. God knows I've tried, but it's impossible to ignore. So let's stop fighting it and enjoy ourselves."

"I want a lot more than just desire from a man. I want him to care. Even if you cared, which you don't, a relationship with you would be short and sweet, and end unceremoniously when the next attraction came along. I'm not going to be one of the nameless hordes who sample your undoubted charms, then vanish into obscurity. I'd rather you remember me as the one who said no." Her voice quivered with pent-up emotion.

He let go of her and stepped back. The anger suddenly ebbed, leaving his face an expressionless mask.

"I thought we'd already established that, Kate. The 'nameless hordes' are just a myth."

How could he be so damn cool, while her stomach churned with sickening pain and disillusionment. But then again, what else had she expected?

"Nevertheless, all you want is a casual fling and that's the last thing I'm looking for."

He gazed fixedly at her, those strange silver eyes revealing nothing, then turned abruptly and walked away. She slumped down into the chair and picked up her coffee, shaking so badly the hot liquid spilled over onto her hand, but she barely noticed the pain. How easy it would have been to say yes.

But saying she didn't want to be one of the nameless hordes had been more than a convenient defense. It reflected her deepest feelings. Well, there was one difference between her and the rest. Given the chance, she had turned him down. Thank God she'd retained enough sense to do that.

Kate walked into Myles's suite with strong misgivings. Why had she let Tony talk her into coming to the postshow party, against all her better judgment?

The sunken living room was already crowded with the usual assortment of beautiful people . . . and Steve. He was chatting lasciviously to a pair of buxom, rosy-cheeked twins. He wouldn't. Would he? Then again . . . if he were a woman, there'd be a four-letter word to describe him. She moved on, making her way through the crush to Tony, standing by the bar.

They had been chatting for a few moments before she noticed Myles, near the French windows, deep in intimate conversation with an exquisitely beautiful woman. Small and delicate, a luxurious mane of auburn curls framed her heart-shaped face. She talked with animation, her blue eyes resting adoringly on Myles's face. He appeared absorbed and fascinated, oblivious to everyone else.

It looked like a meeting of the mutual admiration society. Kate watched them compulsively, her stomach knotting with painful jealousy, yet she couldn't tear her tormented gaze away.

"Gorgeous, isn't she?" Tony had noticed her distraction.

"Yes. Who is she?" Kate tried hard for nonchalance.

"Lise Fremont, a dancer with the Deutsch Ballet. The funny thing is," he smiled, "she doesn't speak a word of English, and Myles doesn't speak French. They're having to communicate in German."

"Funny? More like downright hilarious. Seems to me they're *communicating* pretty clearly without saying anything." The bitchy comment escaped her before she could stop it. Tony's sharp look made her realize she was being far too transparent. The last thing she needed was for Tony, or anyone else, to guess her feelings.

"Kate! Is that you?" came a voice behind her. She turned around, her face breaking into a smile at the sight of a tall, attractive, dark-haired man.

"Adam! What a wonderful surprise. What on earth are you doing here?" The musician and record producer had been one of the first people she'd met in New York.

"I was about to ask the same of you." He grinned, taking both of her hands in his, and kissed her with undisguised pleasure.

She smiled up at him, squeezing his hands in return. "You first."

"I'm mixing an album in Berlin. I just came over for the concert."

She turned to introduce him to Tony, but discovered he already knew Adam Benedict. In the midst of virtual strangers it felt wonderful to see a familiar face and catch up on news of mutual friends.

"Come on, Kate, let's heat up the floor for old time's sake."

She smiled into Adam's persuasive hazel eyes. With a grin at Tony, she let Adam pull her over to the corner where a few couples were swaying to a languorous beat. This was what she needed, a chance to relax with someone who didn't fill her with desire one moment and anger the next.

Laughing at something Adam had said, as they moved together to the music, she caught sight of Myles glaring at them.

Feeling a sudden rash desire to needle him, she put her head on Adam's shoulder and snuggled up close. No matter how petty it was, she felt gleeful satisfaction to see Myles's face pale with tight-lipped disapproval, the china doll beside him forgotten for the time being.

The music stopped and Myles approached. "Adam. Good to see you."

The two men shook hands. Myles was calm and urbane, the perfect host, but Kate saw the dangerous glint of steel in his eyes.

"I heard on the grapevine you might be looking for a new producer, Myles."

"We'll have a word later." He smiled noncommittally, then turned to look at her with a cold anger he didn't bother to disguise. "Can I speak to you for a moment, Kate?"

Her mouth set obstinately. *Fine. Let's get this out in the open.* She let him lead her through the crowd. They slipped unobtrusively into his bedroom, Myles closed the door and leaned back against it. Bracing herself, she turned to face him in the dimly lit room.

"This is none of my business, but I feel compelled to warn you." The fury in his clipped, quiet voice came through loud and clear. "I happen to know Adam Benedict, and believe me, you can't play flirtatious little games with him. You might get more than you bargained for."

"You're right, it *is* none of your business. But just for the record, I, too, know Adam, and perhaps I'll get exactly what I bargained for," she hissed back.

He took a step away from the door, out of the shadows, and she saw his face, narrowed eyes glittering with menace.

"So much for all those high-flown sentiments about not getting involved with a musician."

She stepped back, alarmed by the tightly leashed anger that threatened to explode. Yet she felt the reckless urge to goad him further.

"I'm not planning to marry him."

"What are you planning? A casual, meaningless one-night stand?"

How dare he be so contemptuous after the way he had behaved. "Is that your idea of the only logical conclusion?" she spat out. "You're no better than Steve. You just have a different approach. Why didn't you warn me against yourself?"

"I feel like strangling you, Kate! Is that what you think of me? Well, I'd better start living up to it."

He lunged across the few feet separating them, and before she could react, one steely arm crushed her against him, his mouth claiming hers with such ferocity that her tightly clamped lips yielded to the insistent pressure, forcing her to allow the invasion of his tongue. She despised herself, yet was unable to stop this onslaught of passion.

His hands slid over her, caressing feverishly. Over her swelling breasts, the nipples hardening as he kneaded their taut fullness through the thin cotton of her dress. She sighed helplessly and his lips softened on hers, slowly savoring their parted sweetness, her tongue tasting him in return.

Her fingers inadvertently moved over the hard buds of his nipples. He groaned deep in his throat, sliding his hands down to the curves of her small buttocks to pull her arching against him, leaving her in no doubt of his arousal. With a superhuman effort, she dragged her mouth away from his.

"You son of a bitch," she moaned, turning her face

aside. "Isn't one woman enough for you? Do you need to have us all groveling at your feet?"

That stopped him. He drew back and turned away. She buried her face in her hands. In the strained silence she could hear his labored breathing. She looked up at the sound of his voice, her cheeks wet with silent tears.

"I didn't mean that to happen." He ran a shaking hand through his hair. "Kate, I'm sorry."

He turned back and she saw self-condemnation in his eyes through the mist blurring her vision. Her anger evaporated, leaving her feeling utterly desperate, helpless, prey to her own emotions.

With a stifled gasp she pushed past him out the door. Thankful at no sign of Tony or Adam, she fled the party back to the sanctuary of her own room.

SIX

Kate sat in the departure lounge at Dusseldörf Airport looking out the rain-streaked windows to the lowering gray sky. The weather matched her mood this morning.

Myles and Tony entered through the sliding doors just as their flight was being announced. Despite the dull morning he wore dark glasses, concealing anything his eyes might betray. She couldn't tell if he glanced at her or not as he walked by.

Just after they took off, she looked across the aisle to see him wrapped closely in his trenchcoat, his sunglasses removed and his eyes closed. She noticed the length of his dark lashes resting on his high cheekbones and the shadow of stubble on his jaw. She'd never seen him unshaven. It gave him an oddly vulnerable look, particularly in sleep. No subterfuge. No defenses.

After last night, she had every reason to feel angry with him. Yet she felt overwhelmed by an inexplicable flood of compassion so strong she had to turn away, only to find Tony watching her.

"How can he fall asleep so quickly?" She blurted out the question to cover her embarrassment at being caught staring.

"It's not so difficult if you haven't had any sleep the night before." Tony gave her a mischievous wink. The smile froze on her face. That louse! How could she be feeling sorry for him when he'd been up all night, doing God knows what with his damn ballerina?

Located right on the river Main, the large hotel stood in the very heart of bustling Frankfurt, boasting every convenience. Tony had invited her to go out to lunch and have a look around. As Kate pulled a brush through her hair, she heard the expected knock.

When she opened the door, her smile of greeting faded in surprise at the sight of Myles, clean-shaven and looking his usual elegant self. Dressed casually in olive pants and khaki shirt, he leaned one broad shoulder against the opening and crossed his arms.

"And I'm delighted to see you, too, Kate." He spoke sharply, his eyes narrowed in irritation at her change of expression.

"What are *you* doing here?"

"After that reaction, this will come as a big disappointment . . . I'm afraid Tony won't be able to meet you after all. Something came up."

"Oh, I see," Kate said coolly. "Thanks for letting me know, but you didn't have to go out of your way. A phone call would have done."

"Perhaps . . . but you see I was hoping you'd let me apologize. For God's sake, stop making it so difficult for me. I know I acted like a swine, but short of promising to hang myself, I don't see what else I can do to make amends."

Was he sincere, or did she detect a trace of sarcasm?

"Well, hanging yourself would do for a start." Her voice had a cutting edge as Lise Fremont's heart-shaped face loomed in her memory.

"All right, I promise to do that right after I take you to lunch."

He gave a coaxing smile and her lips curved in unwilling response. What did he have up his sleeve this
time? How could she resist the temptation to find out?
Besides . . . she clutched at the justification that it
would help the article.

"Let's walk down Wilhelm Strasse," he suggested
as they left the hotel, looking reasonably incognito in
the slouch hat and camouflaging sunglasses. "I thought
we'd make our way up to the Zeil. No tourist worth
their salt visits Frankfurt without going shopping."

Kate felt a sudden lighthearted burst of recklessness.
Why was she being suspicious? Why not relax and
enjoy his company?

The broad, pleasant avenues were thronged with people, bare arms and legs soaking up the summer sun.
After twenty minutes of leisurely walking, they came
to the Zeil, a wide pedestrian boulevard. Crowded with
shops, restaurants, and cinemas, weary shoppers packed
the clustered cafe tables in the green shade of hundreds
of plane trees.

Myles never seemed to be the same way twice; she
had grown used to his chameleonlike changes of mood.
But this was the Myles she felt most comfortable with.
Stop fighting it, just enjoy the day. She seemed to be
losing the battle with that little voice of temptation.

All over the boulevard, street musicians entertained
the strolling crowd, from a flautist playing Vivaldi to a
large gray-bearded man cranking an old fashioned bar-
rel organ.

One in particular caught Myles's attention. A skinny
young man in threadbare jeans and much-washed T-shirt
sat under a tree playing his guitar and singing. Myles
paused and smiled, dropping some money into the open
guitar case in front of him.

"Fifteen years ago that was me."

"You played on the street?"

He looked amused at Kate's surprise. "I played anywhere I could make some money. I busked around the streets of London for a while with a couple of other musicians. There's no better way to develop a thick skin. After a few days the insults just roll off your back.''

How could she possibly imagine the urbane, sophisticated Myles, tramping around London playing in tube stations and on sidewalks? "I guess everyone has to pay their dues," she conceded in vague astonishment.

"I won't even tell you about my experiences playing in strip clubs," he said with a mischievous grin.

"Please don't!" Kate laughed. "I'd rather remain in ignorance."

"Excuse me . . . Mr. Hunter?"

They looked around to see a very young girl, possibly ten years old Kate guessed, looking up at Myles with an anxious face.

"Can I have your autograph please?"

He took the small notebook and pencil she held out, then to Kate's complete astonishment got down on his haunches and smiled at the child.

"What's your name?" he asked, pencil poised.

The little girl blushed to the roots of her fair hair and smiled back. "Fredrika." She twisted her ponytail shyly.

He was doing it again. Blowing all her preconceptions. A man who spent his whole life constructing elaborate facades to keep the world at a distance had just betrayed himself in this moment of genuine warmth.

Quickly she took the lens cap off her camera. This was too good to miss. What a perfect picture for the article. She focused in on the expression on his handsome face.

Through the camera lens, Kate watched him listen to the child. Why had she never noticed that quality of attentiveness before? Perhaps because he kept himself aloof from people in general. Although he could be affable when necessary, she was always aware of the restraint behind the smile. Only with Tony did he ever seem himself. And with her, today. Did that mean she'd penetrated the barriers in some way, and hadn't even known it?

She snapped the picture and slowly lowered the camera, feeling like she'd had some kind of revelation. A painful jab between her shoulderblades startled her. She looked around, dismayed to see an excited crowd surrounding them, people pushing each other out of the way to shove bits of paper in Myles's direction.

A tall man elbowed Kate aside, and for a frightening moment she lost sight of Myles. Frantically she fought her way through the unyielding crowd until she finally saw him signing his name with a strained, patient expression.

His eyes locked onto hers through the shifting throng and she could have sworn she saw in them more than just relief at a familiar face. He pushed his way over to her and took her hand, lacing his long fingers tightly through hers. She could feel him trembling and realized she'd been right. He was afraid.

And he had every right to be afraid. Sensing he was leaving, the crowd became insistent, more demanding and volatile.

"Stick close to me." Myles's voice was low and tense as he fought his way through. People began pushing against them and only Myles's painful grip on her fingers prevented them from being separated. Then he was running, pulling her after him, and the chase was on.

They dashed madly down the Zeil hand in hand. Looking back as they darted down a side street, she saw a gaggle of fans in hot pursuit. Startled diners at street cafes looked up in comical astonishment as they shot by, as if the hounds of hell were snapping at their heels.

Around corners, down alleys, through shopping arcades . . . it felt like they'd been running forever. Finally they ran around a corner into a deserted alley and collapsed against a wall.

Kate leaned against Myles, fighting for breath. She looked up at him slumped against the bricks, his head thrown back, eyes closed, panting from the exertion. Suddenly she began to laugh. It was so childish, such an undignified predicament for two adults to be in. Especially suave, urbane Myles Hunter, being chased down the street like a scene from a Marx Brothers movie.

At the sound of her laughter he rolled his head sideways and opened his eyes. "I'm glad you find it so amusing."

"You have to admit, Myles. You sure know how to show a girl an exciting time." She exploded in a fit of giggles and bent double, hugging her aching abdomen.

"It's not funny," Myles protested as he began to chuckle. "Just wait, you'll get tired of it after a while." He pulled off the sunglasses and hat and wiped an arm across his brow, pushing back damp tendrils from his forehead.

"But I won't have time to get used to it, will I?" Kate panted, still trying to catch her breath.

Then she looked up and met a brooding intensity in his eyes that made her smile fade away. They were very close, her shoulder pressed against his arm. Her heart was thudding madly against her ribs, and for one breathless moment she thought he was about to lean down and kiss her. Seeming to check himself, Myles stepped away from the wall and put his glasses back on.

"Let's go and have lunch," he said quietly, walking back out onto busy Lange Strasse and hailing a taxi.

Kate climbed in and Myles swung in beside her, giving instructions to the driver in rapid German. The taxi headed south toward the river. Close beside him in the cab, Kate felt his nearness keenly.

"We're going over the brook, as they say here in Frankfurt," Myles told her. He laid his arm across the back of the seat, his fingers accidentally brushing her hair, sending a shiver trembling down her spine.

"Where?" Kate asked distractedly. Anywhere was just fine with her.

"Across the river to Sachsenhausen. It's the older part of the city."

The river shimmered blue in the warm haze of afternoon as they sped south across the Obermain Bridge. Myles's hand rested beside her shoulder, his leg not touching but so close to hers, she could feel his warmth on her bare thigh below the short skirt. Her heart was still pounding, though she'd long since caught her breath.

"We're more likely to be left unmolested over here," he told her as they got out of the taxi in a narrow, cobble stoned side street. "In this part of town people are more interested in having a good time drinking apple wine. They don't have the energy for harassing tourists like us, they're too relaxed . . . sometimes comatose, in fact," he laughed. " . . . but only after one glass too many."

Charming old inns abounded along the streets of Sachsenhausen, their steep roofs clothed in ancient wooden shingles and a riot of flower-filled window boxes, the narrow irregular streets hung with colorful bunting for a local festival. The images crowded in on Kate, her senses heightened by Myle's nearness.

In the cool shade of a plane tree, in the walled courtyard of an apple-wine pub, they sat at one end of a long wooden table happily eating pork ribs and sauerkraut. The white-coated waiter poured out their apple wine from a blue-and-white earthenware *bembel*. The cider slid down her parched throat—cool, smooth, and delicious.

They sat and talked over their meal, while the crowd around them ebbed and flowed from table to table in warm and friendly chatter. Most of the patrons looked like locals rather than tourists, and Myles responded in German to the friendly remarks from the group of older couples filling up the rest of their long trestle table.

"You speak the language very well." His fluency had impressed her. "Did you study it at school?"

"Only if you count the school of hard knocks . . ." Myles said with a wry smile. "I spent almost a year working grimy little clubs in Hamburg." He paused and took a sip from his glass, staring into it reflectively.

"It's amazing how quickly you learn a language when you have to argue your money out of a chiseling club owner or persuade your landlady to give you one more night in her seedy establishment before she kicks you out into the street."

He said it with a smile, but it was another reminder of the long, hard road he'd traveled to reach this dizzying pinnacle. Nothing had been handed to him on a silver platter. Kate suspected he'd seen more than his share of the sleazy side of life.

No one recognized Myles, who had removed his hat and glasses. Or if they did, they had the good manners not to mention it. He had shed his usual cool reserve, too, and made no attempt to be seductive.

Free of the threatening confusion of sexual pursuit, Kate felt more happy and relaxed in his company than she ever had. As they talked and laughed together, she noticed every little detail. The way he smiled sometimes with a boyish mischievousness she found irresistible. The warm light in his gray eyes when he made her laugh. There was no doubt about it, she really was chipping away at that stony facade.

"I want to hear more about your family . . ." Myles said unexpectedly.

"There's not all that much to tell . . ." Kate hesitated, but he just propped his chin on his hand and smiled encouragement.

So she told him how her hard-working parents had built the small brick house in which she grew up. How her dad took laboring jobs after arriving in Canada until he got his electrician's certificate.

She talked about Sean, and Patrick's nearly completed medical degree, how Maggie was a nurse, working part-time now while the twins were small. She felt she must be going on interminably, but Myles seemed genuinely interested in everything she told him.

Perhaps that one glass of cider had loosened her up. She told him embarrassing family stories, but painting a picture of a home always overrun with friends, full of fun and love.

"What do your parents think of their daughter working so far from home?" he asked suddenly.

Kate shrugged. "They're not thrilled. But they've accepted it. They encouraged us kids to work hard and pursue our dreams. No matter how far from home those dreams might take us, we know we can always count on their support."

"They sound very nice." He looked across the table and smiled, filling his eyes with her.

All morning his gaze had been drifting between the tantalizing swell of her breasts revealed by the scarlet dress that skimmed her tanned shoulders and the brief skirt, showing too much of those long, shapely legs for his peace of mind.

Her chestnut hair glowed with auburn highlights in the shifting sunlight, her luminous green eyes smiled back at him, and his heart expanded with sudden happiness.

She looked young and fresh and full of life and he

liked being here with her. Hearing about her family, he could see more clearly now why she had such an open, caring nature.

"What about *your* family?" Kate could have bitten her tongue the minute the words left her lips.

His eyes went suddenly blank and cold. "I was an only child. My mother is dead. And my father? With any luck, he is, too." His face set into a mask of stone.

The icy dismissal in his voice made her shudder and she remembered that unhappy little boy in the picture. She'd give anything to know more, but not at the cost of seeing Myles disappear again behind that wall of cold indifference. If only she hadn't been so thoughtless. She'd spoiled everything.

"Besides . . . my life's an open book." His mouth twisted with bitterness and he gripped his glass more tightly. "Look in any newspaper, you'll find all the details."

He'd been so relaxed, so open and trustful, treating her like a friend or perhaps even more. He hadn't made a point of telling her it was off-the-record. They'd just been two ordinary people enjoying each other's company. Until now.

"I'm sorry, Myles." She gazed down into her glass, inexplicably angry, feeling somehow personally responsible for every cruel inaccuracy ever written about him.

"She had a very hard life, you know, my mum."

Kate looked up swiftly at his quiet, unemotional words. He was absentmindedly tracing patterns in the condensation on his glass, but she knew he was miles . . . and years, away.

"She slaved away at menial jobs just to keep us going. She wanted me to be happy, to make something more of my life than she ever had."

"It must have been very hard to lose her."

Myles looked up startled, as if just realizing he'd

spoken out loud. Kate's heart ached to see his torment, wanting to comfort him, but not knowing how.

"Yes . . . very hard. It was so damned unfair. She died just before I finally became successful enough to make life easy for her, to repay her for all the unselfish things she did for me." He sat in silence for a while, bitter sorrow briefly etching his face, staring down unseeingly at the plain pine table.

There was nothing to say. Compassionately, she reached out and took his hand. He tensed for a second, then relaxed and gently returned the pressure.

It was dangerous, it was hopeless, but Kate was very much afraid she was falling in love. The more she got to know the real man beyond the mythical image, the more she found herself *caring*, not just desiring.

The rest of the afternoon went by in a golden haze. They wandered the streets together, then walked down to look at the river. She felt content just to bask in his attention, conscious of every little thing he did, catching him looking at her when he thought she was unaware.

All her senses were working overtime today, making her burningly conscious of even the most casual touch. His arm around her shoulder as he turned her attention to the view down the river. The way he took her hand as they climbed the steps to an old church.

It gave her an enthralling secret joy. Perhaps tonight or tomorrow he would be cool and distant again, who could tell? But this memory could never be taken away.

As the afternoon drew to a close they took a cab back to the hotel. As they sped across the bridge, back into the center of town, Myles turned to her.

"Are you going to the promoter's dinner party tonight?"

"I thought it was just for you and the band . . ." She hadn't even thought of going. "And besides, I do have work to catch up on."

"You can always do that another time," his seductive voice coaxed. "I'd like you to come . . . as my guest."

"Thanks." Kate accepted, rather uncertainly. "Actually I suppose this sort of occasion is all part of the tour background, isn't it?"

"Leave the notebook at home, Kate . . . I want you to take the night off."

He gave her a slow smile that made her heart skip a beat. God knows, she had tried to fight this feeling, but had only succeeded in getting in deeper. At the door of her hotel room she paused.

"I've had a lovely day, Myles. Thank you."

"But it's not over yet," he promised. "I'll meet you down in the lounge at eight. All right?" With an enticing wink, he turned and walked away toward his suite.

Kate stood beneath the warm spray of the shower and smiled. *Is he wooing me?*. Did he expect the evening to end in his bed? Somehow all the reasons for denying him had evaporated.

Last night he had been as lost to control as she, making it clear it wasn't just a one-sided attraction. Then today, the pains he took to atone for his behavior made her feel he must care about her in some way. No, she didn't even want to try to analyze this, just let the lovely dream go on as long as possible. . . . Whatever happened would happen.

Riding the elevator down to the main floor at eight-o'clock, Kate caught a glimpse of her reflection in the polished steel door and smiled. She felt like a princess tonight in the white silk dress that showed off her light tan and glossy dark hair to perfection.

Baring her shoulders and close to the body, it flared out softly below the hips into a skirt that swished sensuously around her legs. She felt the essence of chic simplicity, with delicate white sandals and sparkling earrings, her hair in a sleek chignon.

As she walked into the lounge she saw Myles and Tony sitting at one of the small tables. They looked up as she came in and it was intensely gratifying to see amazement on both of their faces as they rose to their feet. Not that she'd been an ugly duckling, but she definitely felt like a swan tonight.

"Kate! You look absolutely fabulous," Tony said as she reached their table.

"Thank you." Kate felt supremely feminine and confident. Myles said nothing, but his eyes traveled over her with slow appreciation more eloquent than any compliment he could have uttered, sliding up to meet her gaze again. The smoldering sensuousness in their depths set off a fluttery trembling inside her.

He'd dressed with deceptive conservatism tonight in a pale-gray silk suit and crisp white shirt, pale-pink silk tie, his blond hair brushed back, saved from intimidating perfection by a few silky tendrils flopping endearingly over his forehead.

"Shall we go?" he said simply, taking her arm as she floated out of the hotel to the waiting chauffeur-driven car at the curb.

On a little side street off Kaiser Strasse in the theater district, they went through a discreet doorway into a softly lit interior of sumptuous elegance. Taupe raw silk walls subtly glowing in the candlelight, the deep bronze velvet banquettes running around the outside of the room enclosed a cluster of tables surrounding a small dance floor.

As Myles ushered Kate through the door, closely followed by Tony, the conversation abruptly died away. For a brief second they could clearly hear the soft background music as all heads turned in their direction, then roared to life again as people surged forward to be introduced.

A tall, thin man in a dark suit approached them with a beaming smile. "Myles! It's so good to see you again." He pumped Myles's hand vigorously. "I hope you're still considering that film deal, I have some people here who are very anxious to talk to you about it."

Myles grinned. "You're a sly fox, Jurgen; you should know better than that. You have to argue it out with Tony, I'm just here to have dinner." He paused and turned to Kate, drawing her into the circle of his arm as he introduced her to Jurgen Freidberger, the concert promoter.

Kate nodded and smiled politely, more conscious of Myles's warm hand gently caressing her waist through the softness of the silk. Almost immediately Jurgen, Myles, and Tony were deep in conversation, and though she tried to follow what they were saying, the progress of Myles's lean fingers up her back to tenderly knead her bare shoulder completely distracted her.

"I'd really like you to come and meet Klaus Schmidt; this could be very beneficial to you, Myles." Jurgen motioned toward a group of men standing at the bar.

Myles looked down at her with a particularly sweet smile. "Do you mind, Kate? I won't be very long."

She shook her head and watched him walk away with Jurgen and Tony and scooped a glass of champagne from a passing tray, but somehow the intoxicating bubbles were superfluous. She already felt euphoric.

Spotting Steve and Paul, she went over to say hello and circulate a little while Myles was busy.

"Hell of an upscale joint, isn't it, Kate?" Steve grinned. It looked like he'd been sampling the champagne for quite a while. "And how about these women!"

Kate looked around to see the crowd sprinkled with the usual supply of striking, glamorous beauties.

"Man, I should do okay now that you've taken Myles out of the running for tonight."

"You make it sound like a horse race . . . or the Olympics," Kate said in disgust, wondering why she was letting an idiot like Steve irritate her so quickly.

"Yeah, but that's for amateurs . . . and honey, I am *no* amateur." He leaned back with a smug grin on his face. "And from what I hear, neither is Myles." Paul had been sitting quietly through all this when he suddenly guffawed loudly and choked on his champagne.

Kate excused herself while they were still enjoying this witticism. Feeling vaguely insecure, she wandered over in Myles's direction, needing to recapture the magic she'd been feeling before Steve's crass remarks.

Engrossed in conversation, she didn't think Myles had seen her, but as she walked by he reached out, put his arm around her shoulders, and pulled her over to join him. While he talked, his fingers gently stroked her skin, the possessive gesture making her feel wanted, as if she belonged there at his side.

At dinner she sat across from Myles, near the head of a long table running down the center of the room. The schnitzel was superb and the conversation lively and amusing. With Jurgen on one side and Oskar Hagen, owner of a large chain of record stores on the other, she didn't lack for attention.

Myles sat next to Jurgen's wife Ilsa, a plump Nordic blonde who spoke little English. Kate noticed him translating some of the conversation so Ilsa wouldn't miss anything.

All through the dinner, Kate had trouble keeping her eyes off him. From time to time she caught him looking at her with glowing appreciation. And once she saw Ilsa's gaze dart from Myles to her and back again in shrewd assessment. She didn't want to let Steve's ignorant innuendo spoil the evening, but it did make her wonder how these people perceived her. Just another in the endless procession of decorative beauties?

Finally the empty dessert plates and coffee cups were being unobtrusively removed when she glanced up to find Myles watching her with hot intensity. Everyone else faded away, and they were alone.

Her breathing came faster, her pulse racing at the unmistakable desire in his eyes. His gaze slid down to focus on her mouth. Her lips felt dry; she nervously ran her tongue across them and saw his eyes darkening, promising what . . . ? A stormy passion? A step into the unknown?

"And how do you think the European Economic Union will affect the magazine publishing business?" The question rudely penetrated the seductive haze surrounding her. She looked around distractedly at Herr Hagen's vaguely professorial face.

"Oh, wonderfully satisfying . . ." she sighed fervently, and quickly realized how inappropriate her reply had been as he stared back at her in confusion.

"Uhm . . . I mean . . . probably positive, I should think," she fumbled.

"May I have this dance, miss?" Tony leaned over her shoulder.

"Yes!" She jumped up and excused herself, leaving Herr Hagen looking faintly bewildered at her hasty retreat. She followed Tony to the dance floor, already crowded with couples moving to the gentle sway of Brazilian rhythms.

"Thanks," she said briefly as Tony's arm encircled her waist and they began moving around the floor.

"For what?"

"Never mind." She shook her head and smiled. "Hey, it's too bad you couldn't make it this afternoon. We had fun!"

"Oh, really? Somehow I didn't think you'd miss me."

Kate wondered at the dry note of caution in his voice. "Why couldn't you come?"

"Myles suddenly found a lot of trivial things that only *I* could take care of."

"Why do I feel you're trying to tell me something?" Tony suddenly looked as if he wished he'd never spoken. "Come on, Tony," she continued. "If you've got something to say, why don't you say it?"

"It's none of my business. I should have just kept my mouth shut. What do you think of Frankfurt?"

"Stop trying to change the subject."

He looked distinctly uncomfortable, not quite meeting her eyes. "Okay . . ." he sighed reluctantly. "The thing is, I think Myles is becoming . . . no, not *becoming, is* interested in you."

She heaved a sigh of relief. "Is that all?"

"Look, Kate, I don't know you very well, but I do know one thing. You're out of your depth with him."

She stopped dancing. Did she feel so offended because it was none of his business, or because the same thought had occurred to her?

"Thanks, but I'm all grown up now, Tony. I know how to handle myself." She looked up into his concerned face.

"You certainly look the part tonight." He gave her a rueful smile. "The cool international beauty, who knows the score and keeps her heart to herself. But that's not really you, is it, Kate?" he said sadly. "I'm just afraid you're both going to end up hurting each other."

"You could be right. But there's no turning back." It was too late now. She loved him.

"There's no future with him, you know."

Her eyes suddenly stung with tears and her throat tightened at the truth of Tony's words. "Yes, I realize that. So you see, you have nothing to worry about."

The music ended and Kate realized they hadn't been

dancing. As they left the floor she quickly dashed away the tears when she saw Myles approaching.

At the sight of Kate locked in Tony's arms, a tear trickling down her cheek at whatever he had said, Myles had felt a red-hot shaft of jealousy pierce him. How could he feel this way about his best friend? But ever since he'd met Kate he'd been acting like a stranger to himself.

"My turn now, I think." He put an arm around her shoulder and led Kate back onto the floor as another song began, to a slow Latin beat.

Then everything else was forgotten as he took her in his arms and they swayed slowly to the music. He gazed into her limpid eyes for a long moment, then pulled her closer until her head nestled against his shoulder and his fingers spread possessively along the curve of her spine. She smelled wonderful. The heat of her body through the flimsy silk was setting his on fire.

"I've been waiting for this moment all evening," he murmured against her fragrant hair. She pulled back a little to look at him and he couldn't bear to have her soft lips so close to his and not kiss her. In an agony of unfulfilled desire, he curved his fingers around her slender nape and brought her head back to rest on his shoulder.

He wanted her so badly, wished he could tell everyone to leave so he could slowly peel away that alluring scrap of silk and kiss every exposed inch of her creamy flesh. He wanted to worship her body with his hands and mouth until the raging torment inside him could only be sated by plunging into her soft flesh, feeling her surround him, draw him inside her.

"Let's get out of here," Myles said in a low, tense voice against her temple.

Kate nodded in mute consent. People would notice, jump to the obvious conclusion, but she no longer cared. Myles wanted her and she wanted him. God, how she wanted him! Every part of her ached for his touch, and all her resolutions had long since faded away.

The song hadn't finished, but she let him lead her off the dance floor. She picked up her bag from the table as they briefly said good night to Jurgen and his wife. In some obscure way she was glad Tony didn't see them leave. He'd been right in all his warnings, but somehow none of that mattered.

She was doing precisely what she had sworn never to do—letting herself be swept away on a tide of emotion that could only lead eventually to a desolate, lonely shore. But how could she resist? How to deny this need inside her that she'd never felt so strongly before? How to refuse this sensual passion she felt in him, all the more alluring for being so hidden under his icy calm.

They stepped out into the balmy night. Kate smiled up at him. "Can we walk? It's such a beautiful evening."

Myles groaned inwardly. He could barely wait to get back to the hotel. But he wanted it to be perfect for her, too. He could wait. But not for too long.

He took her hand. "I know a path that follows the river."

Kate squeezed his fingers; she wanted this dream to go on forever.

SEVEN

The broad, paved footpath hugged the gentle curve of the river, lapping dark and smooth at the stone wall beyond the fence. Softly illuminated by the glow of streetlamps, it was almost empty as she walked with Myles toward the glittering tower of the hotel rising beyond the belt of trees, her hand nestled in his possessive clasp.

Couples and small groups of people passed them occasionally, then suddenly there was no one. They were all alone, the city a constellation of lights that could have been a million miles away rather than a few hundred feet.

A bridge arched overhead. Myles suddenly stopped, pulling her into his embrace, then pressing her against the concrete wall. She shivered at the cold roughness against her bare upper back, the pent-up tension she could feel vibrating in him, the way his sensitive fingers touched her naked shoulders, trailing his thumbs along the ridge of her collarbone with a controlled kind of tenderness.

Her hands reached up to frame his face, its handsome planes thrown into relief by the dim light of the streetlamp. Fascinated by his mouth, her fingers traced the outline of his finely molded lips. She watched them part, his tongue caressing each fingertip with moist heat. Looking up, she met the smoldering passion in his eyes, and knew he must see it mirrored in her own. She felt him tremble in response, exulting in her power to arouse him.

"Kate . . ." he whispered unsteadily. His lips touched hers tentatively at first, as if uncertain of his welcome, lightly kissing each corner of her mouth, then the soft fullness of her lower lip.

Craving for his full possession, she wound her arms around his neck and pulled him closer, her lips parting in seductive invitation, her tongue encircling his, tasting him, reveling in his hungry exploration.

His hands slid down over the swell of her hips, his fingers inching up the silky fabric so he could caress the heated flesh of her bare thigh. Her body twisting sinuously against his hand left him weak and trembling with frustrated need and he felt the savage urge to rip away her clothing and give his hungry touch free reign of her naked flesh.

Incoherent as her jumbled thoughts became, one thing was clear. She wanted him so badly. Wanted to quench the overpowering longing he aroused in her. Wanted him to take her to his bed and give her every ounce of this boundless passion she felt in him.

Suddenly he ended the kiss and rested his forehead against hers with a tortured sigh, then pulled away a little, tracing the line of her lips with his thumb.

"Oh, Kate . . . what am I going to do with you?" His husky whisper broke with emotion.

"Anything you like . . ." she moaned with an abandoned longing she could scarcely believe herself. Her heart ached in an intensity of love. Turning her face into his palm, she pressed her lips against his lean fingers. "Myles . . ." she said in a tremulous whisper,

"I've never felt this way for any man before . . . You do care."

He went still for a moment, then moved abruptly away from her as the cloud of silk slid back down her legs.

Turning his body so she couldn't see his face, he raked trembling fingers through his hair, then stuffed his hands into the pockets of his suit, as if to control them. He turned back to her, his eyes clouded with an emotion she couldn't understand, but a black premonition of despair clutched her heart.

"Myles . . ." Kate stared in dread, "what's wrong, what's the matter?" She tried to subdue the panic rising inside her.

He took a step toward her and gripped her shoulders hard, his fingers digging convulsively into the soft flesh of her arms.

"I don't want you to feel that way about me." His harsh voice cut into her.

"What do you mean?" She could hear the ring of desperation in her words, her mind reeling from his abrupt abandonment.

"I don't want you getting sentimental over me." All trace of desire had vanished.

Where moments before he had burned with fiery passion, now only icy cold restraint remained, as she begged to be understood. "But I can't just make love with someone I don't care about."

He shook her, his fingers biting into her arms. "That's just it. I don't want you to care."

"You have nothing to do with it. You can't dictate my emotions." Her spirit reasserted itself, saving her from groveling despair.

"For God's sake, Kate, don't you understand? I just want to sleep with you, I don't want to set up house!"

With a disgusted motion, she wrenched her arms out

of his grasp and stepped back. What a fool she'd been, deluding herself like that.

"What makes you think I want that, either?" She lifted her chin. She'd be damned if she'd let him see how he'd devastated her.

"Because I know you," he said bluntly. "You'd never be satisfied with anything less than commitment. Well, that's the *last* thing I want."

"I can't believe that."

"Believe it." He paused, then continued with pitying scorn. "You don't get it, do you? It's a game, an amusement. You just don't know how to play it."

"Well, thank you for letting me down gently." She didn't try to suppress the biting sarcasm in her voice. As she turned away from him in blind misery, he stopped her. Gently cupping her chin in his long fingers, he forced her to look at him.

"I just think you should know the score, that's all. I'm not the romantic hero of your dreams, so stop fantasizing about me."

Her throat tightened with emotion at the compassion in his voice. Why couldn't he have remained a cold, callous bastard? He would have been easier to hate.

"You're not the heartless swine you're painting yourself, either." Her voice thickened with unshed tears.

"Whatever you think, here's the way things stand. It's obvious that I want you, but I just want to have sex with you. I don't want to marry you."

Kate flinched at the brutal honesty of his words, but still she persisted.

"If you're as cold-hearted as you claim, why didn't you bring all this up tomorrow morning, after we'd slept together. You know . . . wham, bam, thank you, ma'am!"

He smiled involuntarily. "You're determined to make a saint out of me."

"No, not a saint, merely human . . ." she said

sadly, looking at his face in the dim light. "You're right, Myles. I can't play the game. I don't even understand the rules." She held his troubled gaze for a long time until he sighed heavily.

"It's time for you to go home."

He took her arm, leading her up the stairway to the busy street roaring overhead. Hailing a passing taxi, he put her in, giving the driver the name of the hotel.

As the cab drove off she looked back to see him standing in the glow of a solitary streetlamp, hands shoved in the pockets of his jacket, a lonely figure. Then he turned away, quickly disappearing into the darkness.

Kate shrank back into the corner of the seat and rubbed her bare arms, feeling cold and empty. Worse still, she loved him more. It had come home to her with crystal clarity when he had tried so hard to be despicable. After the first flush of anger, she had felt a strange compassion for his loneliness. Why did he push so hard to keep honest emotion at bay?

Her every instinct urged her to reach out to him, but the barriers were too high. Even knowing how fleeting the solace would be, Kate yearned for him to hold her again, relived with aching intensity the unfulfilled erotic promise of that kiss.

"Hello there, I haven't seen you for a while."

Kate looked around to see Tony walking rapidly up the hallway to where she stood waiting for the elevator.

"Going for dinner?" he asked. She nodded, acutely aware of the last extended conversation they'd had at the party in Frankfurt almost a week ago. A week where she'd done her best to avoid Myles and he'd made it easy for her.

She had concentrated on accumulating background detail, traveling on the coach with the band and crew through the rolling wooded countryside of Germany.

From Frankfurt to Munich, then Vienna, and finally here to the port city of Hamburg.

Tony invited her to join him and as the elevator ascended, Kate wondered how he'd interpreted her leaving the party with Myles.

Huge floor-to-ceiling windows encased the dimly lit rooftop restaurant, giving the impression of a floating island in the sky. Their table overlooked Lake Alster glistening in the twilight.

With the soft piped-in music, and Tony's undemanding presence, Kate began winding down after the exhausting coach trip. He filled her in on the latest news, while she leaned on her elbow and listlessly traced the lines on the snowy cloth with her fingertip.

"We've finalized the film deal with Klaus Schmidt," he told her. "They're going to shoot at the Mocambo Theater in Paris three days after the scheduled concerts, and it's already been presold to HBO, the Euro-SkyChannel, Japan . . ."

Tony paused, and she looked up to find him watching her intently.

"Has he broken your heart already?" he asked gently.

In reply she reached out to take his hand where it lay on the table and squeezed it affectionately. "Thank you, Tony . . . thank you for caring."

His sympathetic look made her feel the need to justify herself. "Nothing happened that night, you know."

"I'm not judging you." He suddenly looked young and earnest. "I just don't want to see you get hurt."

"There's no danger of that." Her smile was brittle. "It seems I don't know how to play the game properly. I can't be detached, can't *act* the part. To put it bluntly, my offer was turned down. So there you are. You can relax . . . dear Tony."

As she went to pull her hand away, he slowly carried

it to his lips and softly kissed her fingers before releasing them.

"Just remember, love . . . I'm always here if you need to talk."

Over Tony's shoulder, she suddenly saw Myles poised in the doorway and her heart lodged in her throat. And then he was joined by a strikingly beautiful woman and it dropped heavily back into her chest.

"Diana Blake," she muttered under her breath, recognizing the actress immediately. Her long silvery hair hung straight and loose down the back of the clinging scarlet dress and she looked every inch a star. It shouldn't be a surprise that he'd find someone else so quickly, should it?

Myles felt someone clutch his arm and turned, startled to find Diana at his side again. For a moment he had been completely consumed by the white-hot anger he felt on seeing Tony kissing Kate's hand.

"Tony, darling!" Diana called out and waved as they approached. Myles looked as if he'd rather pretend they weren't there. Kate felt her face set in a tense smile.

"Great to see you again, Diana; when did you get here?" Tony stood up to greet her. She threw her arms around him and kissed his cheek.

"This afternoon. And let me tell you, Tony, I will never take another plane in my life. It was frightful! Absolutely horrendous! I thought my last hour had come!" she finished dramatically.

Now how could you tell this woman was an actress? Kate felt amused in spite of herself by Diana's theatrical delivery.

Tony introduced the two women to each other. Myles still hadn't said a word, his eyes sliding over Kate as coolly and impersonally as if he had never brought her to the brink of total surrender a mere week before. Her brief glance had revealed a tense, shuttered expression on his handsome face. Kate didn't trust herself to look at him again.

"I'm so glad to meet you," Diana said, giving Kate a speculative look.

"It's a real pleasure, Miss Blake. I do admire your work. I saw you in London last month in that revival of *Present Laughter*. You were wonderful."

It was no polite exaggeration, the brittle sophistication of Noël Coward suited Diana perfectly. In some ways she struck Kate as a bit of a throwback to an earlier era. Not only an excellent actress, she sang quite respectably and danced superbly. In the thirties MGM would have snapped her up.

"Oh for God's sake, darling, *do* call me Diana. 'Miss Blake' sounds so deadly. Just one step away from being a living legend of 'the theatah.' "

She struck a dramatic pose and Kate laughed. A little overpowering perhaps, but it was hard not to like her. Myles merely grimaced impatiently and looked as if he'd rather be elsewhere.

"That's our table over there," he indicated, in a not-too-subtle hint.

"Nonsense, darling . . . let's just join Kate and Tony. You two don't mind, do you?" She was already taking the seat beside Tony.

Even if they did mind, Kate doubted very much if it would have made any difference to Diana. She had all the delicacy of a velvet steamroller.

Myles had no option but to sit down, silent and brooding, beside Kate. Even though she felt excruciatingly aware of his nearness, she knew it would be worse if she had to face him.

Apparently oblivious to the tension hanging over the table, Diana chattered away about the film she was due to start shooting in Italy that September.

"So then I told him . . . Guido, caro mio, it's not the nudity I object to. It's that bloody great snake!"

Every head within earshot whipped round toward their table and the waiter who had just arrived coughed discreetly.

"I'm really awfully hungry, Diana. Do you think we could order now and save these horror stories for later?" Myles asked curtly.

"Sorry, darling." She looked at Kate and winked before burying her head in her menu.

Right from the start she'd sensed Diana's curiosity about her beneath the nonstop prattle. The conspiratorial wink left her confused. If jealousy didn't motivate her interest, what did?

"So, Diana . . . how long will you be here?" Tony asked as the waiter placed their smoked salmon before them. Kate felt herself tensing involuntarily.

"I've decided to be a camp follower for a while, at least until Paris anyway. I want to buy a new wardrobe and Myles has such wonderful taste. What *would* I do without you, darling?" She turned to Myles and touched him, her red nails lingering on his bare forearm beneath his rolled-back shirtsleeve.

Kate looked down at her plate; her appetite had completely deserted her now. She felt more alone at that moment than she'd ever felt before.

"I hope you don't think me too rude if I skip dinner. I'm ready to drop and I don't think I'll last through the meal." She put on a smile, and hoped the dark circles under her eyes would help her sound convincing.

Myles and Tony stood when she did, and with a quick good night she brushed unseeingly past Myles and left.

She just wanted to lie down and go to sleep on something that didn't move. But as Kate sat on the bed and pulled off her slacks, she could only think of Myles and Diana. It was probably better he should be visibly occupied with someone else. It would be a constant reminder not to nurture any pointless hopes.

As she pulled the crisp white cotton nightgown over her head she heard a knock.

"Just a minute . . ." Kate slipped on a bathrobe and pulled open the door to see Myles, his face rigid with anger. He pushed past her into the room without a word. She stared after him, then closed the door and walked toward him, baffled but growing increasingly annoyed.

"What the hell do you think you're up to?" His eyes darkened with cold gray fury.

"What?" Kate gasped, completely at sea.

"Don't insult my intelligence," he growled. "You know what I'm talking about."

She felt her fists clenching of their own accord.

"Why don't you just assume I'm stupid," she ground out slowly between her teeth, "and tell me."

"From now on you're to leave Tony alone."

Kate gaped at him stupidly. Complete disbelief strangled the words in her throat.

"He's a friend of mine, and I don't want to see him used." His eyes shifted to take in the turned-down bed, the discarded clothes on the chair, then back to Kate, barefoot in the thin nightgown and robe.

"I still don't understand what you're talking about!"

"I'm talking about the way you all but threw yourself over the table at him. I'd have to be blind not to see it. And that was exactly what you intended, right?"

His mouth twisted in contempt and she suddenly realized he'd seen Tony's tender gesture. Now he was jumping to a wholly insulting conclusion.

"How dare you!" She stepped toward him, so furious she had to struggle hard to restrain herself from slapping him. "How dare you presume to judge me! What right do you have to say that?"

"I know what you're up to, I've seen it all before. I wasn't born yesterday."

They were only inches apart. She could feel his hot breath on her cheek.

"Oh, really? When are you going to prove it?" Kate yelled back in his face.

"Don't push me," he warned, his voice suddenly quiet, his eyes glittering dangerously.

"Why, what will you do? What will Mr. God's-gift-to women do?" she jeered recklessly. Without warning, he grabbed her wrists in a bruising grip and hauled her against his hard body, the impact almost knocking the breath out of her.

Before she could recover, he pushed her back against the wall, pinning her arms beneath him as she struggled to break free. She fought him to no avail. With grim determination his mouth descended on hers, in a ruthless exploration that sent her senses reeling.

Suddenly she stopped struggling, his mouth no longer hard and brutal. Without conscious thought, she let him pull her closer. His hands feverishly caressed her back and down to the curve of her buttocks, molding her to the length of his taut body, his hardness pressing into her soft belly.

Her trembling fingers slid inside the open collar of his shirt, caressing the strong column of his throat before pushing aside the fabric to expose more of his heated flesh to her exploratory touch. They were kissing now with hot sensuality, lips parting in slow, mutual exploration. All at once, Myles dragged his mouth from hers with a groan of despair.

His hands dropped to his side as he stepped back. Kate suddenly felt ridiculously triumphant. It had been an effort for him to stop, she could sense it. It made her feel startlingly powerful. He stood and stared at her, breathing quickly, his eyes dark with need.

"*I* know what you were trying to prove . . . I wonder

if you do," she gasped, her heart still pounding hard. "What *do* you want from me, Myles?"

"I don't want anything from you," he said in a strangled whisper.

"Right . . . but you don't want anyone else to have me, either," she threw out angrily. "Well, it doesn't work that way. Tony is an adult. He can do what he wants, and you have no authority over *me*."

"You're only here because I let you come." He'd regained control of himself now.

"Yes . . . and why *did* you let me come?"

He froze, his expression a mask. "I had my reasons." His voice held ice-cold mockery.

"God, Myles." Kate felt suddenly tired. "You're so used to having your own way, in your own little universe. You're like a spoiled child. Have you forgotten what the real world's like?" She looked at him in disgust. "Go ahead! Wield your power . . . send me back in disgrace. We'll both know how thoroughly unprofessional your motives are."

She returned his hostile glare full force. There was no way she'd let him intimidate her. Finally Myles broke the frigid silence.

"Tony doesn't mean anything to you, don't allow him to think he does."

"How can you be so sure?" Kate goaded. Myles took a menacing step toward her.

"Do you want me to prove it to you again?"

"All that proves is that you turn me on, physically. It's quite obvious I have the same effect on you. So what! There's more to life than that."

"And does Tony turn you on, too?" The quiet voice held an ominous chill.

"That's none of your business," Kate said quickly.

Even so, she'd as good as answered his question. Was that a triumphant glint she saw in his eyes? She stepped purposefully to the door and opened it.

"Now please go. I'm tired and I just want to go to bed." Myles walked toward her, pausing on the threshold to give her a skeptical look. "Alone," she added, cursing her own need to convince him.

"Don't play games with me, Kate." His eyes were bleak.

"Games! My God, Myles, you're the past master. Why don't you go back to your damned actress, you hypocrite."

She slammed the door after him and slumped against it, so angry she wanted to cry. Damn him! She wouldn't let him do this to her again.

Kate paced the room restlessly, body tight with anger and pain. The travel alarm on the night table said eleven-thirty, still only dinnertime back in Toronto. Impulsively she picked up the phone, then after a moment put it down again. After all what could she say to Maggie?

Just that she'd been stupid enough to fall in love with the kind of man she'd sworn never to get involved with. A man who said he didn't want anything from a woman except sex.

Coming out of the shower the next morning Kate heard the phone ringing and ran dripping into the other room to pick it up.

"Good morning," said the woman on the other end as Kate rubbed at her wet hair with the towel and tried to place the vaguely familiar English voice. "I hope I didn't wake you," the woman continued.

"Not at all," Kate said. If it hadn't been for the sleepless night, she'd have been dressed and out by now. At ten-thirty, who on earth would still be sleeping? Then suddenly she recognized the voice . . . Diana Blake.

"I wondered if you'd like to meet for breakfast? I

really think the only two women on the tour should stick together, don't you?'' she laughed.

Why would Diana invite her? Courting publicity perhaps? But there was something intensely distasteful about sitting across the breakfast table from the woman Myles had just slept with.

''I'd like to,'' she replied coolly, ''but I've got work to catch up on.''

''Oh, come on, you have to eat. Besides, I know lots of juicy gossip you'd love to have for the story.''

Kate had to laugh. In spite of herself, she responded to the friendliness in the other woman's voice.

''Okay, I accept. But the juicy gossip is precisely what I can't put in *this* story . . . so it'll have to be off the record,'' she added with a smile.

Why had she instinctively taken a liking to this woman, when any normal person would be feeling furious jealousy? It was hard to say. Whatever the reason, her curiosity had got the better of her.

''Wonderful! Shall we say half an hour, in the lobby?'' and Diana rang off.

EIGHT

"Darling, I'm embarrassed to admit knowing anyone that long. But it's been fifteen years. I was waitressing at a little coffee house at the time . . . between engagements, you know," Diana confided with an ingenuous grin. Then it faded to wistfulness. For a second the actress seemed miles away from the umbrella-shaded table at the little outdoor cafe on the shore of Lake Alster. "And there was Myles. Perched on that tiny stage singing his heart out."

Kate tingled with suppressed excitement. Was this the key to finally unlock his mysterious past? And from the most unexpected source.

It had seemed too Noël Coward for words. Breakfasting with the mistress of the man you were in love with. It was a role Diana Blake could have carried off with aplomb. But Kate still felt dazed at the way the other woman's charm and warmth had captivated her when she should be hating her guts.

"But the songs . . . the songs were beautiful. They were so idealistic and full of hope. The dreams of a young man . . . We were all so very young then." Diana sighed.

And where had that young man gone? Where along the way had he lost his hope. Kate thought of the cynical, lonely man she had left standing under that lamppost.

"Did . . . did you ever meet his mother?" In spite of her best intentions not to pry, she was desperate to know more.

"Oh, heavens, yes, I was a constant visitor, I practically lived there. Of course, Mrs. Hunter was terribly old-fashioned . . ." She giggled. "Oh, my dear, the elaborate tricks we had to resort to, just to get the flat to ourselves. But Myles was such fun. Up to any lark." Diana paused, and took a bite of the buttered roll.

Myles? Up to any lark? Kate just couldn't reconcile that image with the restrained cynicism of the man she knew. What had life done to him, and where did Diana fit in Myles's life now? What about his wife? What about all those other women? Her mind was in turmoil with a million questions begging to be answered. But the subject was taboo . . .

"Fortunately," the actress continued, unknowingly satisfying Kate's curiosity, "our great romance ran out of steam after a couple of months, before we'd reached the screaming stage, so we've remained friends ever since. I love him dearly."

"Not many people can manage that." What an understatement. Kate couldn't believe what she was hearing. Could this be the same Myles Hunter who said he was only interested in sex from a woman?

And another question occurred to her. If Diana wasn't involved with Myles, then why had she invited her to breakfast? That "only two women on the tour" excuse didn't hold water for a minute. Kate had assumed the real reason to be Diana's interest in sizing up a potential rival.

But her complete lack of malice had ruled that out from the start. However, the actress was clearly curious, and Diana had obviously been talking to somebody about her because she'd let slip her knowledge that Kate had lived in New York.

Who had Diana been talking to? And why had they been discussing her?

"I've been very lucky to have him as a friend. Without Myles I'm not sure I'd have got over a couple of rough patches in my life." Diana crossed her long legs elegantly and carefully dabbed the corners of her mouth with the pink linen napkin.

Myles, a shoulder to cry on? A supportive, empathetic friend? Far from answering questions, Diana had just created a million more. Who was this man?

"Of course, hardship was no stranger to Myles. He had a pretty rough childhood." She pulled out a silver compact from her bag and began making minute adjustments to her already flawless complexion. "Mrs. Hunter worked as a charwoman, you know, barely making enough to keep body and soul together. She made Myles finish school, but he turned down a university scholarship so he could start working and take the load off her shoulders. Even then, he was desperately worried about her frail health."

Kate stared out at the lake glittering in the sunlight. The little sailboats began dissolving into smears of white against the blue water as her vision clouded with tears. Who was she to judge him? When had she ever known poverty or the burden of responsibility at such an early age? It made her feel almost guilty about her relatively carefree youth.

"I gather he was fairly young when his mother died," she murmured.

"Yes, and *she* was only forty-four," Diana sighed. "The terrible irony is, she needn't have died. She was on this horrendously long waiting list for a heart operation on the National Health. Only a year later Myles would have had the money to get her into a private clinic. But his success came too late.'' She shook her head. ''It's been eleven years now, but, you know, he's never been the same person since.''

Kate thought of the unutterably sad look in his eyes when they had talked of his mother in Frankfurt.

Diana continued. ''He was so bitter then. In a rage with the whole world, blaming himself needlessly for not doing more. He's so prone to do that . . .''

''How terrible,'' Kate whispered, compassion for Myles welling up inside her.

Staring out at the lake, shimmering in the already blistering heat of midmorning, she felt a physical ache, to think of the pain he must have endured. And then to lose his wife so tragically. It went a long way toward explaining that tangible sense of loneliness he seemed to carry around inside. *Oh, Myles. If only you'd let me love you.*

''Oh, my God!'' Diana looked at her watch as Kate sat up with a jerk. ''I have to meet Myles in half an hour and he *hates* to be kept waiting.''

''Don't I know it,'' she said with feeling.

Firmly refusing Kate's offer to split the bill, Diana pulled some notes from her Chanel bag and tucked them under the plate.

They walked into the lobby in time to see Myles stepping off the elevator. Her heart lurched painfully with love.

Just seeing his tall, lean figure striding across the lobby, she wanted to walk into his arms and feel his lips on hers again. And she'd hold him and love him and try to make up for all the pain and anguish he'd been through. If only he'd let her.

But after that scene last night she'd be lucky if he'd even speak to her.

At that moment his eyes met hers. She caught a brief flash of some nameless emotion in their troubled depths, but then they hardened. That shuttered look she had begun to hate so much veiled his eyes, telling her more eloquently than words to keep her distance.

As he approached, his gaze shifted to Diana, then quickly back to Kate. He faltered, then continued on with a smile that froze her blood, a humorless curve of his mouth conveying nothing but anger and contempt.

She couldn't face that smile. Why wouldn't he look at Diana? Oh, God, not another scene. She hated herself for her cowardice, but she just couldn't handle another confrontation.

Diana glanced at her watch with feigned nonchalance as Myles reached them. "Goodness! Is it that time already?" Her throaty laugh sounded gay and discordant in the tension-filled silence Kate felt so keenly. "Just give me a few minutes while I run up to my room . . . and don't give me that offended look. You know very well it doesn't work on me."

Diana sauntered away, and Kate made a dash to follow her, but didn't get ten paces before his peremptory voice stopped her.

"Kate . . . a word with you?"

Keeping his temper in check had taken every ounce of control Myles could muster, when what he really wanted to do to that conniving little muckraker was wring her neck.

He stalked into the lounge, making no effort to shorten his stride as Kate tried to keep up with him. She tripped and stumbled and he managed to stifle the automatic urge to reach out and help her just in time. She could fix her own damn shoe.

He strode on ahead, hardly noticing the handful of people scattered along the bar, and made his way over to the deserted corner by the grand piano, where a grouping of potted palms offered some privacy. He stopped, turning to face her abruptly, and she cannoned right into him.

Her hands automatically reached out to steady herself

against his chest, starting a fire where they burned into his flesh, spreading lower to blaze hot and intense in his loins. He gripped her wrists and pushed her back, hating the way his body reacted to her merest touch.

The impact had jolted the breath out of Kate for a moment, but the brief contact left her quivering with reaction long after he'd pushed her away.

She forced herself to face up to the anger darkening his eyes. After all, what could he do to her? That is, as long as she didn't lose her temper. Again.

He couldn't see a shred of remorse in those bold green eyes, if anything, they blazed defiance, and he felt a powerful urge to see her squirm.

"So, tell me . . . what did you have for breakfast, Kate? A fat, juicy morsel of scandal?"

So that's what this was all about. He thought she'd been pumping Diana for information! She held her breath and counted to ten. She'd never met anyone who could rouse her temper as quickly and easily as he could, but that didn't mean she had to let him.

"Now just a minute." She held up her hand as if to ward him off. "I know it must look pretty bad, Myles, but you're making a mistake . . ."

He stiffened. If she thought her trembling voice and pleading green eyes would soften him, she'd soon find out how wrong she could be. Not this time. He'd been too lenient with her. It was time she realized just who held the reins of power.

"You're right; I've made a lot of mistakes, starting by letting you come along."

She hated that cold contempt in his voice. It was easy to believe she meant nothing to him at all. How could she even begin to convince him she could be trusted. "Myles, I really think you should hear me out before you say anything else you'll regret."

"Hear you out . . ." His cold laughter sent a chill

up her spine. "I'd find more truth in the *News of the Globe*."

Kate's face burned. How dare he sneer down his aristocratic nose at her! God, she was sick and tired of his insulting innuendos about her profession and the implication she was a low-down, conniving snitch.

"Damn it, Myles, I've never lied to you! You have no right to accuse me of that!" If anything, she'd been too painfully honest.

"And you have no right digging into my personal life, and that includes whatever you dredge up from my friends. You must think you're very clever, worming your way into the good graces of everyone close to me. First you have Tony eating out of the palm of your hand, now Diana. Well I'm warning you. I'm on to your little game."

Any lingering compassion she felt for him had long since vanished. Every muscle in her body clenched tight with anger as she moved a step closer to him, the words deceptively calm. "Exactly what is my little game?"

"Oh, come on. Taking Diana out for a cozy little breakfast chat. What exactly did she tell you?"

"Let's get a couple of things straight." Her voice had risen, and a few heads at the bar turned curiously in their direction. She lowered her voice, but the anger came through. "I didn't take Diana. She took *me*! And what makes you think we were talking about you?"

"You must think I'm an idiot. What else could you possibly have been talking about?"

She was so incensed by now, the fact that he was right didn't enter into it. "This may come as the surprise of the century to you, but the whole world does *not* revolve around Myles Hunter! And furthermore," she began to emphasize her words by jabbing her finger repeatedly into his unyielding chest, "I'm *sick* of your ego, I'm *sick* of your accusations, and I'm bloody well sick of *you*!"

Her furious words fell into the suddenly silent space between them. Kate stared up aghast at his face drained of all color, a pulse beating frantically by his mouth, his eyes burning down into hers.

"Oh, really?" It took every ounce of willpower he possessed to keep him from reaching out and wringing her neck. Never in his life had he ever met anyone who could get him as blazingly angry as this green-eyed bitch. "Well then, I'll put you out of your misery, shall I . . . You can leave. *Now*. There'll be no story."

He had the satisfaction of seeing her blanch before he turned on his heel and left her. But in the twenty seconds it took to storm out of the lounge and into the busy lobby, his satisfaction had turned to dust. He stopped in front of the huge plate-glass window and stared unseeingly at the busy street outside.

His eyes had begun to burn. His throat felt tight and painful. Oh, God, what was she doing to him? He hadn't felt like this since the nightmare of Alison's funeral. He raked a hand through his hair, a feeling of despair overwhelming him. *He'd* given her the power to do this by opening up to her, against every instinct of self-preservation.

But in spite of it all, even now at the height of his anger and frustration, he wanted her. How often had he imagined running his hands over every inch of her silky, fragrant skin, over the firm swell of her breasts. He hungered to feel her taut nipples hardening in his mouth, to taste her feminine sweetness with his tongue until she shuddered and moaned softly in his arms. He wanted to drive deeply into her soft flesh, feel her wrap those long, slender legs around him, urging him to an ever more frantic rhythm until he spilled his seed inside her.

He spun away from the window with a frustrated groan and swore under his breath. Why did he torture himself like this? He could have had her if he hadn't been so damn scrupulous about her feelings. If he'd just made love to her, he'd be free of this agonizing need. That's all it was, the lure of forbidden fruit.

Desperate to distance himself from these dangerous fantasies, he strode over to the elevators just in time to see the black doors slide open and Diana emerge.

She carefully scrutinized his face, then sighed. "I knew it. I knew when you phoned and asked me to come and be your bodyguard."

"Diana, I'm not in the mood." He suddenly felt disillusioned and bone-weary.

"I knew it as soon as I met her . . ."

"If you're through with your crude attempts at psychoanalysis, let's get going."

"I can see this is going to be an absolutely enthralling afternoon."

He followed her out through the revolving glass doors, throwing one last look back toward the doorway of the lounge. Kate hadn't emerged yet. What was she doing? Was she all right? Oh, damn. What did he care. She was nothing but trouble.

He should be feeling victorious, she was finally out of his hair. So why did he feel like someone had stuck a knife in his gut? A cold bleak chill settled over his heart like a shroud.

For a long time after Myles's angry exit Kate stood immobile, staring at the doorway through which he had disappeared. She would never see him again. What had she done?

Fighting down the panic and despair threatening to overcome her, she sank into a nearby chair and buried her face in her trembling hands, willing herself not to burst into tears. Intellectually she'd been prepared to leave in another week, but the reality of being forced to go so precipitately was more than she could cope with.

On the heels of this numbing thought, Kate suddenly

remembered what should have been her first consideration. What about the story? How could she go back to Bob and tell him she'd lost it? What reason could she give?

Sorry, Bob, I acted worse than any fawning groupie. I didn't just want the guy to sleep with me . . . I wanted him to love me, too. She could just imagine his pithy response to that excuse. She'd broken all her rules with Myles and it should be a bitter lesson.

The enormity of the situation overwhelmed her, until a feeble hope flashed into her mind.

"Tony. Something terrible has happened. You've got to help me!"

She had finally tracked him down swimming lengths in the hotel pool. Dragging him away from his exercise, Kate perched on the edge of a lounge chair and proceeded to tell him what a horrible mess she'd made of things.

". . . And now I'm trying to decide between two equally dreadful alternatives. Either going home in disgrace to face Bob, or groveling for Myles's forgiveness. Although I doubt that would do any good. You know him, Tony, what are my chances?" The words had come tumbling out so frantically she could only hope they made sense.

He dried off his chest with a towel, a small, thoughtful frown creasing his forehead. "I'll tell you what. Why don't I see what I can do. Pouring oil on troubled waters is my specialty."

"Darling! I'm so glad you've decided to join us."

At least Diana was her usual effusive self. After that first quick glance at Myles when she'd joined them at their table in the rooftop dining room, Kate hadn't had the nerve to look at him again. That shuttered look veiled his eyes and she had no way of knowing what he was thinking.

How had Tony worked this miracle? All he'd said over the phone was, "Everything's okay, come and join us for dinner."

But what did that mean? Nervously, she screwed her starched white napkin into a crumpled ball in her lap. She couldn't tell anything from Myles's impassive face. Had he forgiven her? Did he feel any regret for the way he'd behaved?

God knows she owed him an apology, but she wanted to wait for a private moment.

"I don't know what you said to Myles this afternoon, but he's been an absolute bear all day," Diana complained.

Kate felt like covering her head with the crisp white damask tablecloth, but she couldn't help looking up to see Myles's reaction. She found him watching her with a hint of mocking amusement lurking in his silvery eyes.

"You do like to exaggerate, Diana. I was perfectly civil," he drawled, his gaze never leaving Kate's face. "I was just getting over the discovery of my own insignificance in the overall scheme of the universe."

Kate winced and felt her cheeks burning. She looked down at the menu to avoid his eyes.

Diana laughed. "So you put him in his place. Well, good for you! Someone has to from time to time."

Why wouldn't someone change the subject? Kate shot a pleading glance at Tony.

He caught her look. "Well . . ." He cleared his throat and picked up the menu. "What's everyone going to have?"

Kate smiled at him gratefully, then caught Myles watching her through narrowed eyes.

By the time she'd finished the last of her delicious veal Prince Orloff, she felt more relaxed than she would have thought possible when she stepped off the elevator. She could sit back and enjoy the softly lit romantic atmosphere, the candlelight reflecting off the gleaming silverware, the sparkling crystal, the fairy lights of the city spread out below as if the stars were at her feet.

For a moment a feeling of heady unreality washed over her. Here she was, little Kate O'Brien from Toronto, dining with two internationally famous stars in these glamorous surroundings.

Any minute she expected Robin Leach to step out from behind one of the marble pillars with his microphone and bray, "When the rich and famous Myles Hunter dines out, he does it in style. And take a look at this million-dollar view. It's enough to make your champagne wishes and caviar dreams come true."

Kate fought down a giggle. No doubt about it, this jet-set lifestyle was beginning to take its toll on her mental health. She dabbed at her mouth with her crumpled napkin to cover her smirk and caught Myles watching her expressionlessly, then raise a sardonic eyebrow.

"I know . . ." Diana declared loudly as the waiter came by with the dessert trolley. "After this, why don't we all go to the Reeperbahn for a little fun?"

"I don't think that's a good idea. I'm sure Kate wouldn't like it." Tony looked over at Kate for confirmation.

"Why wouldn't I like it? What is it?"

"It's one of the most blatant red-light districts in Europe," Myles explained, as if even the most ignorant hick should be familiar with the name. "Tony's right, you'd be shocked to the core. Bad idea, Diana."

His sophisticated condescension got under Kate's skin. "I've lived in New York City, it takes a lot to shock me. Who do you think I am, Snow White?"

"No . . . I thought you were Sleeping Beauty," Myles responded quietly, the intimate expression in his eyes telling her he was thinking of that moment in the square. Kate felt her heartbeat speeding up as she held his look. Tony and Diana looked mystified.

"My, aren't you being protective, Myles. That's not like you at all," the actress piped in with a sly wink at Kate, who found herself wishing Diana would get laryngitis.

"Shut up, Diana," Myles said patiently.

After dinner they took a taxi from the hotel out to the St. Pauli district west of the old town, and got out on the notorious street known as the Reeperbahn.

The sweltering day had turned into a steamy night. After the air-conditioned comfort of the hotel, Kate could already feel sweat beading down her spine in the hot-house atmosphere, her thin white cotton dress beginning to stick to her skin.

Diana took Tony's arm and walked on ahead, leaving Myles strolling, hands in pockets, beside Kate.

Under the garish glow of countless neon signs, they joined the surging crowds that ebbed and flowed along the broad avenue. Club after squalid club opened its doors onto the crowded street beneath the lurid glare.

Myles said nothing, but now and then she caught a sidelong, amused glance and knew her face must betray her repugnance. None of her experiences had prepared her for this kind of blatant depravity. In the seamy underside of the port city, all the entertainment had one common denominator—sex, in its most carnal form. Walking through these sordid streets made her feel thoroughly revolted, yet morbidly fascinated.

In the wake of Tony and Diana, they turned down a dim, narrow side street.

Myles gave her a sidelong look. "This is the Grosse Freiheit, or Great Freedom . . . which is a phenomenal understatement." He gave her a wry smile. "The Beatles and I shared a venue. That seedy joint over there." He indicated a cold blue neon sign pointing down a filthy flight of stairs. "Not at the same time, however."

Roughly dressed men stood in front of the lighted doorways, yelling coarse encouragements at passersby. Kate edged closer to Myles, feeling very insecure. She'd lost sight of Tony and Diana and wanted to make sure she didn't get separated from Myles. The place made her flesh crawl. Stories of white slavery and forced drug addiction flashed through her head.

"It hardly seems possible." Myles had stopped, looking around him in disgust. "But I think it's even worse than . . ."

Kate looked up to see him staring fixedly over her shoulder. Even in the garish neon glare, she could tell his face had drained of color. Turning in bewilderment, she found a seedy-looking man behind her. His eyes were on Myles and Kate shuddered at the repulsive smirk on his narrow face.

"Bet you never expected to lay eyes on me again."

His rasping cockney sneer made her uneasy, and she instinctively shrank back against Myles, wondering who the man could be. All she knew was that he gave her the creeps. She longed to get away from him and was thankful when Myles put his arm around her shoulder, pulling her protectively against his side.

Obviously the man's appearance was just as disturbing to him. She could feel his fingers biting painfully into her soft flesh and his voice sounded harsh and cold above her.

"What do you want?"

The man smiled unpleasantly. "Now, now . . . Is that any way to speak to your old dad?"

NINE

Kate gasped and looked at Myles for confirmation, but apart from the painful pressure of his fingers clutching her shoulder, he seemed to have forgotten her presence. His eyes glittered with a mixture of hate and disgust. She felt his rigid body trembling as he glared at the man standing grinning in front of him.

"Aren't you pleased to see me, Son?"

"Not particularly," Myles bit off and turned away, but the other man moved in front of them.

"What's the matter? Think too much of yourself to be seen talking to your father?"

His insinuating, mocking voice sent a cold shiver creeping up Kate's spine. As if in a distorted mirror, she could now see the chilling similarity between Myles and this dissipated human wreck. In the chiseled aristocratic features, now shrunken, gaunt, and deeply lined. But the pale-gray eyes, so disturbingly like Myles's, held a shrewd, cunning gleam that made Kate uneasy.

"How the hell did you find me anyway?"

"Followed you, didn't I? From that fancy hotel of yours. Didn't think you'd end up in my part of town."

"It doesn't surprise me to find you in this sewer. It's

152

where you belong." The harsh, uncompromising words and the loathing in Myles's voice made Kate go cold all over. He sounded like a stranger.

The older man laughed, unabashed, displaying rotten, uneven teeth. "You always were an arrogant bastard. But then you get that from your mother's side, don't you? How is the old bitch these days?"

In a flash, Myles had let go of her and grabbed the other man by the frills of his pink nylon shirt, pushing him backward with murder in his eyes. "You filthy swine, how *dare* you even mention her name!"

Kate stood openmouthed in horror at the scene before her. Myles with his fists tightly clenched, his chest heaving, looking as if he wanted to tear the man apart. And the older man making a show of being unaffected as he straightened his cheap suit. But his crafty eyes never left Myles's face.

"Tell you what." He ran a hand over his dark slick of pomaded hair. "You could have me out of your life completely for a small investment of fifty thousand pounds. Chicken feed for someone like you."

"Go to hell." Myles's soft measured words were filled with venom.

The older man shrugged. "Like your old sod of a granddad used to say . . . Nothing ventured, nothing gained. God, he was a stupid bastard."

Myles turned away from him, and for the first time since the whole encounter began, his eyes met Kate's. The anger, the hatred, the bleak misery she saw there made her heart ache. What could she do or say? He reached for her elbow and pulled her along with him.

The raucous voice followed them. "You never did tell me what you were doing down here, Son. Looking for something kinky, were you? Something that nice little tart you have there won't do for you?"

Kate felt sick. Myles continued to walk, stiffly ignoring the taunt, maintaining an iron grip on her arm until they were out of the seedy side street and back on the main avenue of the Reeperbahn.

She had to say something, had to let him know that she was in complete sympathy with the way he must be feeling. "Myles . . ."

"I don't want to talk about it. Furthermore, I don't want *you* to talk about it. Ever. To anyone. Understand?" His hard voice cut into her as he scanned the crowded pavement ahead, obviously looking for Tony and Diana.

"I would never, *ever* talk to anyone about this. It's your private business. I told you before, you can trust me."

"Trust!"

Kate jumped at his explosive outburst, blinking in confusion as he spun her around to face him.

"Where the hell have you been all your life, wrapped up in cotton wool? Look around you! Would you survive a hell-hole like this for two seconds if you trusted people? You slay me, Kate . . . you and your high-flown principles, your utopian dreams. How can you work in this industry and not understand? People use each other to get what they want. That's the rotten truth. If you're smart you can do it without getting hurt. Wake up. See the world as it really is, not as you'd like it to be."

"There you are, you two." Diana's musical voice floated over the crowd that flowed around them, like a stream around a rock, oblivious to Myles's white-hot anger and Kate's bewildered hurt.

Just before Diana and Tony reached them, Myles repeated in an undertone. "Remember . . . not a word."

"Tony and I want to go dancing," Diana called out as they got closer.

"No, Diana, *you* want to go dancing." Tony spoke with tolerant amusement.

"Count me out," Myles said emphatically, and waved down a cab. "I'm tired and I have a show tomorrow night. I need to save my energy."

"Gosh, darling, you are becoming a boring old twit," Diana said pityingly. "I remember when you could dance all night and still be full of beans the next day."

"Unlike you, Diana, I won't be pampering myself by spending tomorrow in bed." His face was drained of all emotion and his voice sounded flat and expressionless.

They piled into the taxi and sped north, dropping Diana and Tony off at the Blauer Satellit Disco, in the deluxe Hamburg Plaza Hotel on Marseiller Strasse. Myles and Kate continued on alone back along the lakeside Alsterufer to their own hotel. In the dim interior they sat carefully apart, the silence hanging heavily between them as Myles stared out the window.

Her mind was still reeling from the shock of their encounter with his father. No wonder he was so cynical and distrustful of relationships. Who could blame him?

Compassion welled up inside her, overwhelming the ever-present sexual awareness. She just wanted to move over and put her arms around him, but how could she without revealing the depth of her love.

"How's the article coming?" The unexpected question sliced into her thoughts abruptly. Kate turned to look at him. "Almost done," she said, then added tentatively, "Except for one very important interview."

"Yes . . . I've been thinking about that." He was silent for a moment, staring out the taxi window at the darkened lake, distractedly tapping his lip with his forefinger. Then he turned and gave her a careful look. "Shall we say tomorrow afternoon, about one?"

Kate's eyes widened in surprise. "Tomorrow?" she said vaguely, unable to believe what she was hearing. "Wonderful . . . thank you."

They had arrived at the hotel. As they walked into the lobby, Kate preceded Myles through the revolving glass doors, still in shock over his unexpected agreement. After everything that had happened between them she'd given up hope of ever getting the interview.

"Why?" she asked, as they waited for the elevator. "What made up your mind?"

"I remembered my responsibilities." He stared at the black doors in front of them. "And I realized . . . that I behaved very badly this afternoon and I'm sorry about that." The doors slid smoothly open and they stepped inside.

"Yes, I'm sorry about that, too . . ."

Myles continued as if he hadn't heard her. "Of course, I'm assuming you're not so sick of my ego that you can stand to hear me talking about myself for a couple of hours." The corners of his mouth lifted in a strange little smile.

Kate felt a guilty warmth rushing to her cheeks. In her self-righteous anger that afternoon she hadn't been completely honest.

"Okay . . . we *were* talking about you, damn it!"

"I know." The dry amusement in his voice made her feel even more of a fool. "It's so easy to appeal to your conscience, Kate." He gave her an incorrigible smile and she had to smile back at him. He'd done it again.

She chalked up an imaginary score. "Another point for Myles Hunter."

Kate returned his measuring look, and felt a strange happiness. In some way they'd returned to the playful bantering she had enjoyed so much, the exciting sense of being an even match.

"I shouldn't have lost my temper." She lowered her eyes.

"And I've been very wrong." The elevator stopped and they stepped out on Kate's floor as Myles went on, the humour vanishing from his voice. "I've been wrong all along. I'm sorry about last night. I have no excuse, except that . . . I was jealous of Tony, and I still am. I should never have let our relationship become personal."

Kate stopped fumbling with her key in the lock and stared at him in complete astonishment. *Jealous?*

"Why are you telling me this? You aren't making it any easier for me."

He leaned one shoulder against the wall by her doorway. "You're a beautiful woman, Kate."

Her gaze dropped to her hand on the doorknob. She couldn't bear to face that gentle finality in his voice.

"You deserve to be loved by someone who can give you what you need. You *should* be in love but . . ." The words trailed off to a tortured whisper.

"But not with you." Kate couldn't keep the bitterness from showing as she finally looked up at him.

"But not with me," he repeated resolutely.

"You can't change the past now, Myles," she murmured. Or banish her feelings that easily. After letting herself in, she watched his lengthy stride as he walked back to the elevator.

How could she be in love with such an enigma? Once again, just when she began to think she understood him, he had left her completely baffled.

The thought of Myles in the shower, water coursing down his lean, muscled body, made her mouth go dry. Kate wandered restlessly around the luxurious hotel suite, hardly noticing her surroundings. She wished Tony had stayed after letting her in. He could have distracted her from the disturbing pictures he had unknowingly sent racing through her mind.

Absently running her hands along the gleaming ebony contours of the Bechstein grand piano, her thoughts strayed to Myles and what he might be doing right now just on the other side of those pale-gray bedroom doors.

She felt far too vulnerable and disturbed, imagining his hands, those lean, sensitive fingers lathering soap over the strong curve of his shoulders. Perhaps he had stepped out now, water beading on his tanned skin, had reached for a towel and begun rubbing slowly down his body, his hard chest, his firm, ridged stomach. Kate closed her eyes for a second. How could she be this aroused when all she'd done was imagine? Of course, she could always stop imagining and walk through those doors into his bedroom right now.

Desperate to distract herself from that dangerous path, she dropped her bag onto one of the overstuffed pink chintz loveseats, put her tape recorder and notebook on the heavy glass coffee table, and stepped over to the window.

Three tall, uncurtained casements looked out on the wrinkled surface of Lake Alster spread shining below, dotted with lunchtime sailors.

An antique mahogany desk stood before the center window, a guitar leaning against one side and an open notepad lying on the intricate inlaid top. Her pulse quickened. Was he working on a song?

Unable to resist, she stepped closer and read, in Myles's quick slanting hand.

"I could be the lover you've been waiting for.
I could ruin everything for you."

Kate caught her breath. A chill tingled through her. Was it a warning? An omen?

"Poking through dustbins again?"

She turned, startled to see Myles leaning against the doorway, arms crossed, a small smile on his lips.

With a groan, she covered her face with her hands. "Oh, God, I give up. I might as well leave right this minute."

Running a hand through the damp blond strands, his teasing smile broadened. "I didn't think a hotshot reporter like you could be put off your stride that easily. You never have been before. Don't disappoint me now, Kate."

There was something boyish and vulnerable about him right now, barefoot in old jeans and comfortable black sweatshirt, his hair still slightly damp from the shower. As usual, she felt overwhelmingly aware of his physical presence so close to her. Always there, it tingled beneath the surface, threatening to flood over if she let down her guard.

"Shall we sit down?" He waved toward the couch, so much the charming host she felt completely disoriented.

Kate had fully expected him to treat the interview as a distasteful obligation, a way of easing his conscience for yesterday. Instead he seemed tolerant and relaxed in a way that completely confused her expectations.

She sat at one end of the loveseat, and Myles lowered himself beside her, a mere foot away, turning his body to face her and curling his legs up under him, looking as amused as she felt flustered. In one brief glance she saw a smile that spoke devilment and sent a shiver of apprehension down her spine.

She picked up her notebook and crossed her legs tightly. If it had been difficult before, it was getting impossible now that he was close enough for the clean scent of soap on his warm skin to assault her senses.

Myles smiled to himself. He was making her uncomfortable and he knew it. It gave him a sense of power. Now it was her turn to discover how it felt to be eaten up inside with frustrated desire. To want someone so badly you couldn't think straight anymore. In spite of his resolution to maintain a professional relationship, he'd been tormented with dreams so vivid there was no escape even in sleep.

He stretched his arm along the back of the couch and allowed his fingers to brush the vulnerable nape of her neck, exposed beneath her ponytail, and watched fascinated as all the little hairs responded to his touch. He saw the telltale blush in her cheeks as she jolted forward and began fumbling with the switches on her tape recorder.

Was this his idea of remaining impersonal? God, how would she be able to think straight when she knew he was being so deliberately provocative?

"You've gone to great pains to get me in this position, Kate. Now what are you going to do with me?"

There was that sand-on-velvet voice again, and that warm, seductive glow in his smoky eyes guaranteed to turn her into a babbling nincompoop.

"That's it! I've had enough!" She jumped to her feet.

He looked up at her, all confused innocence. "Is that it for the interview? Well, that was certainly painless."

"Don't you play innocent with me! You know exactly what I mean. You're doing it on purpose, aren't you?"

With a bewildered shrug of his shoulders he said, "Whatever I'm doing, I promise to stop, all right? Now come and sit down. Relax. You're all tense." He patted the cushion beside him invitingly, but his virtuous act didn't fool her for a minute. The devil still lurked in his eyes.

Kate stepped around the table and sought the safety of the matching loveseat on the other side. She refused to be a victim of his little cat-and-mouse game.

An incorrigible boyish grin broke across his face. "I never took you for a coward, Kate. But if you feel more comfortable over there, by all means."

Giving him a look that had been guaranteed to get her younger brothers to tow the line, Kate picked up her notebook and authoritatively punched the record button. "Shall we begin?"

He uncoiled his long legs and sat forward, elbows resting on his knees, his teasing eyes never leaving her face. "I'm all yours."

His finely molded mouth curved in a slow, suggestive smile so incredibly sexy it brought to mind a world of erotic possibilities that had absolutely nothing to do with the interview.

With superhuman effort, Kate dragged her mind away from the intoxicating visions of what that mouth could do to her body and back to the job at hand.

She'd fix him. She'd show him he wasn't the only one who could be disconcerting. Hit him with a question guaranteed to make him squirm.

"Considering your background, how did you come up with this 'aristocratic young man of a bygone era' routine?" With exaggerated condescension, she indicated the quotation marks in midair. "I mean, did you try on a few other approaches until you found one that worked? The Bruce Springsteen blue-collar hero bit, or the leather-and-chains punk, Billy Idol look? Maybe high heels and purple spandex, like Prince? I mean, did you just keep trying on different hats until you found the one that sold the records?"

Take that, mister. She got a gleeful satisfaction from wiping the smile off his face and watching his eyebrows rise successively higher at every outrageous suggestion. That got him where he lived. In all the interviews she'd read in preparation, he would become very defensive at the merest hint that his image was contrived.

He sat back and mulled over his answer, watching her all the while, sitting across from him in her loose khaki shorts and red tank top. With her hair in a pony-

tail she looked all of fifteen. An unconvincingly innocent fifteen at that.

The calculating little . . . He'd bet his life she knew
how much the question would bother him, and damn
it, it did. Being made to sound like such a fraud by the
press was bad enough, but that Kate should doubt his
authenticity was the last straw.

"You know, I'm sick and tired of this damn question
about my image. I wear what I want. I write what I
want. Being successful is great, but I will not prostitute
myself just to sell records. I am who I am."

"But don't tell me the success hasn't changed you.
No one could remain untouched by the mass hysteria
that attends your concerts. You must know you're the
star of a few million sexual fantasies."

"Including yours, Kate?" he inquired softly, half-
teasing, half serious.

"Let's just stick to the subject, shall we?" She stared
back resolutely, her voice strictly business.

He nodded his head with an ironic glint in his eye
and continued. "Believe it or not, I never set out to be
anybody's idol. I just wanted to make a living at what
I enjoy doing . . . no, what I *need* to do, which is to
make music. I hate this Myles Hunter I see in the newspapers and magazines. He's not me. I hate all the adulation, the need to create an idol. The public impose an
image on you. God help you if you don't live up to it.
And God help you if you start believing it." He smiled
ruefully at her. "I'm damned if I do and I'm damned
if I don't . . . So, what about you, Kate? Do you have
a pet theory about my image you'd like to trot out now?
Believe me, I've heard them all."

His gray eyes were direct and serious as he held her
gaze. She felt a spasm of guilt. Everything he said was
true. Yes, she'd had her theories, some of them reflected in the questions on her notepad she couldn't
bring herself to ask now. But there was one burning

question she had needed answered ever since that first kiss.

Suddenly she reached over and clicked off the machine. Myles raised an eyebrow in surprise.

"Just tell me one thing. If you don't believe in love or commitment, and all you want from a woman is her body in your bed, then how do you come to write lyrics like . . . 'Give me back my stolen dreams, I need the mercy I seek in your eyes . . . I come to you with no defenses, needing the protection of your love'." She held his gaze in silence for a moment. "So where do these beautiful words full of romantic longing come from, Myles?"

He took a deep breath and slowly let it out as he leaned back against the couch and put his legs up on the coffee table, regarding his feet for a second with abstract calculation.

He looked up. "You're the amateur psychoanalyst . . ." She caught the triumphant gleam in his eyes. "Why don't you tell me?"

Kate paused. Why not? After what had passed between them she had the right to understand.

"First of all, I don't believe you write only what sells. A few minutes ago you told me you write to please yourself." A quick gray glint told her she'd struck a nerve. "You're an artist at heart, Myles. You write from your soul. That's why it has authenticity."

"So what, in your humble opinion, makes me tick?"

She ignored his mockery. "I think you try very hard to be cynical, but your songs show me a man with an overwhelming need for love and closeness, yearning for something lost, hoping to find it again. Afraid that if you ever do find that love, you'll destroy it."

He gave her a long, cool, measuring look. The silence hung between them. Then he swung his legs off the table, leaned forward, and switched the tape recorder back on.

"Next question?"

Nothing marred the smooth blandness of his face, but Kate knew she'd got to him. Despite all the barriers, she had begun to discern the real person underneath.

Flipping over a few pages in the notebook, she began asking a series of nonthreatening questions about the rigors of touring and the music on the new album. She noticed him visibly relaxing, losing his watchful air. Finally Kate clicked off the tape, satisfied with the ground they'd covered.

"Thanks. I hope that wasn't too painful." With the recorder safely stowed in her bag, she stood up. "There is one last question I'd like to ask you."

Myles rose from the couch and they stood facing each other across the small, square table.

"Why did you really agree to this?"

The two feet of space between them suddenly crackled with electricity as she met his eyes, feeling the professional pose dropping away.

Now the recorder was off, there was no one listening. She was alone in a room with the man she wanted beyond all others, beyond all reason. It would be so easy to take one step around that small barrier and press her yearning body against his.

As if reading her thoughts, he stepped around the coffee table until he was so close to her she had to tip her head upward to look at him. His warm, clean fragrance filled her senses.

"I've been asking myself that same question." His low, husky voice caressed her spine. A drumming filled her ears she only half recognized as her own heartbeat. The room suddenly became very quiet and very warm. It was time to leave.

Then Myles reached out and gently stroked the downy curve of her cheek. She trembled, mesmerized by his featherlight touch as he lowered his head.

With infinite tenderness he began depositing gentle, teasing kisses against her softly parting lips as he'd been wanting to do for the past hour, until he couldn't bear the torment of denying himself what he hungered for so badly. With a groan, he gathered her pliant body into his arms and finally took full possession of her tempting mouth. He felt her shudder and part her lips eagerly to the thrust of his tongue, the taste of her moist sweetness sending hot, urgent desire shooting through him.

Her arms stole around him as naturally as breathing, and she gave herself up to the insanely blissful embrace. She smoothed her fingers over his freshly shaven cheek as she had wanted to ever since he walked into the room, then tangled them in his damp hair, inhaling the intoxicating scent of soap and subtle aftershave. There was no resisting his sensual onslaught. She was drowning in the sea of her own emotions, her heart hammering painfully against her ribs.

He could feel her breasts flattening against his chest as she pressed herself even closer, her hips moving gently against him, knowing she could feel the throbbing response of his body to every voluptuous brush of her tongue on his.

He slid his hand into the low-cut armhole of her tank top until he found her bare breast. Aware of nothing now but the maddening, urgent need to explore her ever more deeply, he groaned softly, kneading the silky fullness, feeling her nipples tightening in response to his questing fingers.

She gave a shuddery moan and arched against him, driving him to such a peak of aching arousal, it was all he could do not to pick her up and carry her to his bed.

Kate felt an invading flood of warmth surge between her thighs, inflamed by his sure fingers until she thought she would go mad. She ached to touch and stroke his flesh, to taste him, to possess him. Impatiently she pushed his sweatshirt up, dragging her mouth away from his, to trail moist kisses over his smooth, muscled chest.

"Oh, Kate . . ." he gasped against her hair. "We can't fight this any more. It's what we've both been wanting, been dreaming about. Let's not worry about tomorrow. Let's just take what we can get today."

His tortured words slowly penetrated the sensuous haze, and Kate raised her mouth from his skin. Cold despair invaded her heart. "No . . ." Her throat tightened in an agonized whisper and she shook her head.

"You know we've both wanted this since the first time we kissed. Kate . . . I want you so much . . ." he murmured as she drew away, his eyes clouded with desire.

This had to stop now, while she still had the strength. "I want you, too, Myles, more than you can possibly imagine. I want to see your face beside me when I wake up in the morning and go to bed with you every night. But you're wrong if you think that I want you to marry me. And I'm not asking for forever. But I want you to love me, not just desire me."

"I can't . . . I just can't." His dull voice killed any shred of hope she might have had.

She dropped her hands and stepped back. It cost her dearly to let him go, but it would break her heart to pour out her love to someone who didn't want it. She turned away and picked up her bag from the table. Myles hadn't moved from where he stood.

"I've got all I need for the article now," she said slowly, feeling numb. "After Paris I'm going to head home."

"As you wish." His voice was void of emotion.

She barely trusted herself to look at him, but when she did, she saw a proud, solitary man, hardly betraying a trace of the passion they had just shared.

There was no point in hoping anymore. Myles would never let anyone get close enough to love him. She turned and walked out, her throat hurting with the effort of holding back her tears, leaving him standing in the center of the room, alone.

Amid the hot updraughts of a June heatwave, the early-morning flight to Paris bumped and lurched in the turbulence. The headache Kate had woken with worsened with the altitude. Hiding behind dark glasses, she avoided everybody, thankful Myles sat out of sight a few seats ahead.

The tour checked in at the discreet nineteenth-century Hotel Bretagne in the heart of Paris, just off the Champs Elysee and she headed straight for bed, closing the heavy brocade drapes against the late-spring sunshine and pulling the cotton sheet over her head.

Exhausted from no sleep the night before, she lay inert, her head throbbing, until she felt the aspirin finally begin to take effect. As the pain eased she felt herself drifting, reliving the past three weeks in a jumble of confused images.

A rhythmic sound reverberated in her head. She groaned. Oh, God, the headache was coming back. The sound got louder. Suddenly she realized someone was knocking at the door and she'd been asleep.

Throwing off the covers, she stumbled over and turned the handle, feeling cold, crumpled, and bleary-eyed.

"My God, you look like death warmed over." Diana peered at Kate and shook her perfectly groomed silver head.

"Why don't you really try to depress me, Diana," Kate mumbled, pushing her tumbled hair out of her eyes.

"I'll do better than that." She ignored the sarcasm and swept into the room, undeterred. "You're going to change and put on some makeup. We're going to a party."

"You're insane."

Kate closed the door after her and winced at the glare when Diana flicked on the bedside lamp. What time was it anyway? She blinked at her watch and saw seven P.M. She must have slept for hours, no wonder she felt so groggy.

"What are you wearing?" Diana opened the mahogany wardrobe and clucked with disapproval to find it empty.

"I'm not going." Kate slumped down on the bed and watched uncaring as the other woman flipped open her unzipped suitcase and started pulling out clothes, shaking them out and giving each dress a critical perusal.

"Kate, darling, I simply won't allow you to miss this one." Diana laid three dresses out on the bed and stood deliberating over them with a frown. "A floating barge on the Seine . . . the Eiffel Tower by moonlight. How impossibly romantic!"

"Maybe that's a good reason to miss it," Kate said, still feeling too wrung out to even protest this blatant invasion.

"Yes," Diana pronounced with finality, picking up one of the dresses. "The little black one. Chic, understated, definitely you, Kate."

Her victim shot her a jaundiced look. "Yeah, it'll go with the circles under my eyes."

Diana slipped the dress onto a hanger, put it in the wardrobe, then turned to Kate. She folded her arms and tapped one immaculate Chanel pump on the Persian carpet with an imperious look of command reminiscent of Elizabeth the First.

"Kate . . ." Steel glinted beneath the cultured velvet tones. "Hit the showers. You're going to this party and I won't take no for an answer."

TEN

"Cheer up, everybody. We're going to a party, not a funeral!"

Diana was giving it her all, drawing out the vowels in a hilarious send-up of her plummiest West End delivery, but to no avail. The teasing words disappeared uneasily into the muffled silence inside the sleek limousine nosing its way through the Paris traffic jams toward the barge anchored at the Quai d'Orsay.

Myles shot a brief look of concern toward Kate from the opposite seat, then looked away. She bit her lip, carefully smoothed the slim, strapless black dress over her bare legs, and turned toward the window, wishing for the hundredth time she hadn't let Diana bully her into coming.

She should be feeling enthralled, not miserably impervious to the scene outside. Above the buildings ahead rose the impossible steel cobwebs of the Eiffel Tower, looking too much like a postcard to be real. Toward the west the gray sky shaded to delicate rosepetal pink, then deeper peach where the sun's pale disk showed intermittently through thinning rifts in the clouds. In an hour it would be setting and bring some relief from the heat of the day.

At last the limousine pulled up at the quay and they all stepped out into the humid evening. Colorful bunting decked the barge from stem to stern, along with hundreds of lights glimmering weakly in the fading daylight. It looked rather squat and prosaic to Kate's eyes right now, but when darkness fell she knew it would sparkle in a million reflections on the water.

Myles escorted Diana up the gangway, Kate took Tony's arm and fell in behind. White-coated stewards opened a set of brass double doors and the roar of voices inside spilled out into the open air. A hundred faces looked up expectantly, then Myles descended the four shallow steps into the lounge and the babbling crowd swallowed him up.

Winding through the silk-clad throng in his wake, through clouds of heavy, expensive perfume, Kate felt claustrophobic and miserable.

A short, heavy man in navy pinstripes turned toward them. "Tony!" He pumped his hand vigorously. "Looks like Myles gave us another winner. We made the *Billboard* Top Ten this afternoon!"

Tony introduced the president of Ragtop Records, just arrived from Los Angeles. The same man who, according to the industry grapevine, was on the verge of dropping Myles from the label. But now that the tour was an indisputable success, producing record album sales, he was all smiles and ready to lavish Myles with attention. Maybe hoping he'd forget their doubts about his career, now he was hot again and his recording contract up for renewal. Oh, yes, she knew this game all right.

The nuances, the calculated moves . . . Usually she found it all fascinating, but right now Kate felt desperate to escape. She lagged behind, then wove through the crowd toward the doors in search of fresh air.

Myles watched her ascend the few steps to the open doorway, then walk down the deck past the lounge windows. He felt unaccountably worried. She looked so pale, so subdued, not her usual unstoppable self at all. He excused himself and headed for the door.

He found her on the empty upper deck, leaning over the railing and looking down to the few feet of oil-slicked water between the barge and the quay.

He leaned on the railing a yard away from her. "What do you see down there?" he asked dryly. "My lifeless body floating on the sewage?"

Kate turned toward him with a wan smile.

"Or would you prefer me to make it really dramatic." He pointed toward the Eiffel Tower, floodlit now against the dark sky. "I could go right to the top and throw myself off."

Her smile still didn't reach her eyes, but it broadened a little and she straightened up, turning to face him with her back against the railing. How he wanted to take her in his arms, kiss away that sadness. He steeled himself against the impulse and kept his distance. It would only make things worse.

"You have to understand . . ." He struggled for the words. How could he make her see it was better this way? "I decided a long time ago I didn't want to hurt anyone, or have their pain on my conscience. That's why I was honest with you yesterday. But I've done the very thing I wanted to avoid. I've hurt you, and God knows I never wanted that to happen."

She squared her bare shoulders and lifted her chin valiantly. "You stars are all the same, hogging the credit. I'm not going to let you get away with it. I had just as much to do with it as you."

Her bravery cut him like a knife. How typical of Kate. Strong, beautiful Kate. "Arguing now, are you? That's more like it. You really had me worried today.

I didn't think Diana would be able to talk you into coming.''

Something in his tone made her wonder. ''You wouldn't have had anything to do with her paying me a visit, would you?''

To her amazement she saw a flush spread along his cheekbones. *He's blushing!* Clearly uncomfortable, he evaded her eyes. She saw his gaze fasten on a huge old Rolls just pulling up on the dockside, where cars had been disgorging a steady stream of partygoers.

''Good heavens, it's Roddy!'' Myles exclaimed. ''He's heir to some little principality near Liechtenstein, I can never remember which one.'' He spoke a little too quickly. ''You'd never know he's Queen Victoria's great-great grandson. At parties his specialty is dancing naked through famous fountains. He only has the Trevi left to go, but so far the Italian police haven't been very understanding. Strange though, because—''

''Myles Hunter, you big phony!'' Kate cut in. ''Forget your dissolute playboy friends! You sent Diana to see if I was all right, didn't you?'' Myles remained silent and kept his gaze averted. ''Don't try to tell me you don't care.''

''I care, I suppose,'' he said finally, still not looking at her. ''Just as I would for any friend, like . . . Diana or Tony. No more, no less.''

Kate shook her head sadly. ''Who hurt you so badly that you're this scared of love? Was it Alison?'' For the first time she broached the taboo subject. ''I know what the papers said, but I never gave that much credence, especially now that I know you. I don't know what happened but . . .''

''No. You don't.'' Cold and defensive, he retreated behind the barricades. The shutters went down and she despaired. ''Alison is dead and gone. The past is a closed book.'' And one he never wanted to reopen.

"Myles, you old sod! There you are!" A slightly slurred voice wafted up to them.

Startled, Kate looked down to the gangway and saw a young man in evening clothes with a woman on each arm and another hanging on to his neck.

"Come on down and help me entertain these lovely ladies," he yelled up. "I couldn't decide so I brought one of each. What are you in the mood for? Blonde, brunette, or redhead? This one's a real tiger. Grrrr . . ." He growled and nuzzled the redhead in the ear until she shrieked with laughter. With a bottle of champagne in one hand and his bow tie half undone, he looked like he'd been partying since yesterday.

"I'd better join him before he disgraces himself completely," Myles's sigh didn't disguise the wry humor lurking in his eyes. "I promised his father, the Prince, that I'd keep an eye on him."

"His father the Prince?" She folded her arms against her chest and gave him a skeptical look.

Myles shrugged and beat a hasty retreat down the stairway to the lower deck. More likely he just wanted to get away from the situation, from the mention of Alison. From her.

Kate stood at the railing for a few minutes, inhaling the scent carried on the warm breeze. Paris by night. A whiff of diesel, the smell of the river, but she liked to imagine she could detect something of the French *campagne*, lavender and violets from the *parfumeurs* fields to the south.

She sighed. It was just her imagination. Like all her crazy hopes about Myles. She had better go back to the party. The tropical sultriness of the air stirred her blood in a way she found much too disturbing. She took a deep breath, rallying her defenses. *Stop wearing your heart on your sleeve*, she told herself sternly.

Myles watched Roddy and the redhead stumbling all over the dance floor at one end of the lounge to the throbbing beat. How he wished the party were over. How he wished that boy would stop drinking so much and grow up.

Roddy's blonde and brunette had attached themselves like limpets to each arm. Myles tried to make conversation, but all he could think of was Kate.

He couldn't tell her about Alison. But damn it, he did feel guilty about hurting her. He could see her now coming back into the lounge, making a valiant effort to hide her feelings.

She was too sweet, too open and giving. She deserved so much more. It would be better if she hated his guts than to eat her heart out over him. Much better.

He saw Kate looking his way and turned to Roddy's blond friend with a smile of practiced charm.

"You know, Myles," she traced a suggestive forefinger down his shirtfront and simpered, "I've been waiting a long time to meet you."

He hated her thick, musky perfume. Maybe if he pretended it was Kate's delicate fragrance he could stand it. If he'd ever put on a facade, this had to be the most difficult one he'd ever assumed.

Kate watched him leaning over the beautiful blond. Smiling . . . laughing now. She felt pierced to the heart. Myles glanced over at her with a shrug. What's a man to do? he seemed to say.

How could he possibly care? Why was she even bothering to try to look as if she were enjoying herself? Something finally broke inside her, her eyes blurring as she fought back the tears.

Bruised and desperate, Kate sought escape, pushing her way heedlessly against the flow of people. Snatches of conversation hit her ears—games, pretenses, artificiality. All this glitz and glamour and not one shred of real human feeling among the lot of them. She didn't want any part of it, or of Myles.

How could he go so quickly to another woman? How

could he care even as a friend? Why go on torturing herself? She only wanted to get away from the terrible pain inside her. Away from Myles.

Oblivious to the fairytale lights of the city, Kate sat, numbed, during the cab ride back to the hotel. It took every ounce of willpower to keep the tears of despair at bay until she finally reached the sanctuary of her room.

Hot and anguished, they spilled over, running down her cheeks as she collapsed against the door, her body wracked with painful sobs. An urgent knock sounded behind her. She ignored it. The knocking turned into banging, shaking the door.

"Kate! Open this door."

Myles. She took a deep, shuddering breath. "Go away," she moaned, her voice thick and distraught. The knocking resumed more vehemently.

"I'll keep on pounding until you open this door, Kate. Let me in."

She threw open the door. He stood there, fighting to regain his breath, hair windblown, tie loosened, torment in his darkening eyes. Through her tears, she stared in distress.

"What do you want from me, Myles?"

"I want my sanity back." His voice cracked with emotion.

"What do you mean?" she whispered, a seed of hope beginning to quicken inside.

"Can't you see for yourself what you're doing to me? I can't go on like this any longer, Kate," he groaned, his tortured face naked with emotion. "Even my music can't fill the empty space inside me. I need you."

He needed her. The seed of hope exploded to fill her with joy.

With a small cry, she rushed into his arms. Myles kicked the door shut behind him, his lips descending on hers with a famished passion she returned with wild abandon, an admission of desires too long repressed.

His hands ran over her in a frenzied urgency of possession. His soft moans punctuated the silence, echoed by her own responsive sighs, inflaming her even more, making her strain against him, wanting him, wanting to be consumed by him.

"I can't believe you're here!" she gasped against his lips as he pulled away for a second. "Tell me this is real."

"This is real all right. You're in my blood." The admission sounded almost bitter. "I can't stop wanting you no matter how hard I try, no matter how much I tell myself it's a mistake." His voice softened, his long fingers framed her face. "I behaved like a bastard tonight, hurting you that way."

She didn't need explanations. The miracle of him admitting that he needed her was enough.

"When you ran out, it was more than I could bear. I was terrified I'd never see you again. I had to come after you," he murmured, raining soft, moist kisses over her cheeks, her eyelids, with such maddening delicacy she thought she would go insane with frustrated need for the full possession of his mouth.

"And it's more than I can bear that you keep talking, when all I want you to do is shut up and kiss me."

He'd been deliberately going slow, prolonging the exquisite torture of denying himself, knowing that heaven was just around the corner. But the passionate demand in her voice was his downfall, intensifying the throbbing ache in his loins. He couldn't delay any longer when she pulled him down to her and claimed his lips fiercely, taking his breath away.

She clung to him, their tongues entwining in sensual exploration, her body hot with aching desire, feeling him stir in response to the touch of her trembling fingers on the buttons of his shirt. Impatiently she pushed the fabric aside to allow her greater access to his hard, muscled chest.

With a gasp, he dragged his lips away from hers, she could feel his heart beating beneath her massaging palms, mingling with her own frantic pulse. He was breathing rapidly, cheeks flushed, eyes glazed with passion.

"If we don't stop now . . . I don't think I'll be able to . . ." He gave a violent shudder as her questing hands found and caressed the undisguised hardness of his arousal.

"I don't want to stop . . . I want you to make love to me," she whispered desperately. "Now . . . right now. I need you!"

"You have to understand, Kate. I need you, too. I care for you. But I can't give you any guarantees . . ." She kissed away his anguished plea, her mouth molding to his hard, sensuous lips, her tongue inciting a response from him that left her shaken, an enervating warmth spreading between her thighs.

"I don't care . . . It doesn't matter," she gasped against his lips.

She was right, nothing mattered now, except his burning need to fill her, to possess her completely.

He lifted her slender, pliant body in his arms, carrying her over to the bed. Dark and smoky with desire, her green eyes never left his face. He slowly set her on her feet and once again his mouth descended on hers, exploring its honeyed sweetness, as his fevered hands slid down her back. She arched against him, moving her hips against his hard, aroused flesh in a sinuous motion that was driving him wild. *Don't rush*, he told himself. He wanted to savor every touch, every taste.

"Kate . . ." he murmured against her mouth, his soft, husky voice a sensual caress.

She felt the mood subtly change. No longer frantic

and anguished, now it was heated and throbbing with the shared knowledge that nothing could hold back the consummation of their desire.

Unerringly, his fingers found the tab of the zipper on her dress, propelling it smoothly downward. He slowly peeled the strapless black sheath from her slender curves, revealing small, perfect breasts, the rosy nipples enticingly taut, the feminine curve of her waist and hips, her belly, slightly concave above delicate black lace briefs, finally allowing the dress to slip down her long, slender legs and fall in a crumpled pool around her ankles.

Her beauty transcended every expectation, every fantasy. The ache of arousal turned into painful urgency. "God, you're beautiful." The words escaped him on a shaky breath.

Kate quivered under his hungry gaze. His fingers trailed lightly up her arms, over the curve of her shoulders; she shivered at the sensuality of his touch. His lean, sensitive hands brushed over her breasts, swollen and aching now in unbearable anticipation. At his touch she gasped, intense pleasure searing through her veins like wildfire, her breath coming quickly through parted lips. His palms cupped her lightly, his skillful fingers teasing each tightly budded nipple into aching hardness.

Through half-closed eyes she watched him sink to his knees before her. She made an inarticulate sound, her legs weakening in anticipation, and put her hands on his shoulders. His tongue slowly circled each swollen peak in delicious, maddening torture until she could bear it no longer, arching closer, her hands tangled in his hair in silent urging. With a soft groan, he opened his lips, taking the nipple into his mouth, drawing on it with a hot, moist suction as she pressed his head against her with a whimpered moan, melting in an intensity of pleasure until she thought she would go mad.

Myles was straining for control, listening to her

sounds of pleasure, loving the way she tasted in his mouth, her flowery fragrance filling his senses. He buried his face in the valley between her breasts.

"I love the smell of your flesh, Kate, I love everything about your body," he murmured against her damp, heated skin.

She felt his lips moving lower over her belly, his tongue circling her navel. She dug her fingers into his shoulders at the delicious torment and looked down at him. The sight of his blond head against her pale skin was so unbearably erotic, she felt her knees weakening.

His mouth moved lower until it reached the barrier of her black lace panties. With his hands cupping her buttocks, he tugged at the offending scrap of silk with his teeth, then with a groan of frustration his impatient fingers ripped away the delicate fabric.

Her low, husky laugh throbbed with sensuality. "You shouldn't have done that," she whispered shakily, "they were new."

He looked up at her, his eyes glazed with passion but edged with a provocative glint, his mouth curving into a knowing smile. "Do you want me to stop?" His fingers trailed up her sensitive inner thigh, then began slowly teasing the delicate core of her womanhood.

Shaken and trembling under the sensual onslaught, her legs dissolved and she sank to her knees, molding her body against his with a moan. The rough fabric of his jacket scraped across her sensitized nipples with an unbearably tantalizing thrill.

"You do and I'll kill you," she murmured against his mouth, and their lips fused once more in a searing kiss.

Myles impatiently shrugged off his jacket, while Kate quickly disposed of his shirt and tie before her hands went to his buckle.

He felt his heartbeat accelerate at her delicate touch on his skin. With a tantalizing smile in the depths of her emerald eyes, she began unfastening his belt and slowly undoing his trousers, pressing them down around his hips. Her gaze dropped and the hot desire flaring in her eyes at the sight of him filled him with a wild surge of pleasure, a primitive feeling of masculinity. Her gentle fingers closed around him, slowly brushing over his rigid flesh with such arousing delicacy she was driving him wild. Yet every time he thought she had brought him to the brink, she drove him on to even greater heights.

With a groan, he stood and pulled her roughly to her feet. Holding her away for a moment, his eyes hungrily devoured her body.

"You're a devil, do you know that? You've put me through hell and you're trying to drive me out of my mind, aren't you?" he murmured hoarsely, his chest heaving, his handsome face flushed. Every nerve on fire, Kate thrilled at the power of her feminine potency to inflame him like this.

Tearing off the rest of his clothes, he pulled her against him once more, as if unable to bear the momentary separation of their bodies, and tumbled onto the bed.

His arms tightened around her as he covered her face with kisses, murmuring incoherent words against her lips. Winding her hands in his silky hair, she clung to him, loving the heat and strength of his lean body against hers, the unbearably sensual excitement of skin touching skin as their limbs intertwined, rolling over and over in the blindly urgent need to be absorbed into each other. His hands wandered over her, exploring, caressing, until every inch of her body trembled and burned with feverish need.

Flooded with love and desire, she wanted to know him completely, in a way she had never wanted anyone else. While her hands caressed him, her lips made their own bold exploration, over the strong, muscled curve of his shoulder, his chest, loving the scent and taste of his golden flesh.

Passionately, she brushed her lips over the flat plane of his stomach with a teasing, featherlight touch and felt his body stiffen and arch as if inviting her to caress him more intimately. A sheen of fine sweat broke out on his skin, her tongue delicately ran over him, tasting salt.

With a rapid expulsion of breath he pulled her up to take her mouth again in hungry desperation. His hands slid up the length of her thighs to gently squeeze the downy curves of her buttocks before gliding between to caress the warm moist center of her femininity.

She gasped at the convulsive surge of pleasure rushing through her and deepened the kiss, pushing her tongue into his warm mouth more insistently. But it wasn't enough. She wanted all of him.

Suddenly she pulled away and moved lower to take his taut male nipple into her mouth. At the same time her fingers closed around him and began to gently stroke his satiny-smooth skin. His hoarse cry mingled with the soft moans issuing from her throat.

"Kate, do you know what you're doing?" He gave a shuddering groan, his hand reaching to tangle in her hair.

"Uh huh . . . but if you want me to stop . . ." she murmured with feigned innocence.

"Wretch," he gasped, and moved against her.

Kate laughed softly and bent her head to run her tongue across the hard peak of his nipple, awash in the ocean of sensuality he had unleashed in her. There were no boundaries, no inhibitions. She wanted to give him everything.

He pulled her up to capture her lips again, his mouth tasting her, his tongue sweeping languorously into every secret corner, her body quivering and melting in a flood of sensuous warmth as his fingers rhythmically massaged her in the most intimate of caresses.

With a moan of exultation, she moved her hips in mindless response to the hot, silky touch, sinking the fingers of her other hand into the tight, muscular curve of his buttocks, knowing the wild, sweet pleasure of their mouths and bodies fusing. The feverish delirium escalated inside her, in wave upon wave of flaming ecstasy until she couldn't hold back for another second.

On the crest of this delicious agony, Myles brokenly gasped her name and urgently moved his hips between her thighs.

"Myles," she whispered raggedly, her eyes swimming with love, trying to focus on his face.

He slid into her, burying himself to the hilt in her soft flesh as she arched her hips up to meet him and wrapped her legs around him. He met her eyes, clouded with passion, piercing him for a moment with a sense of ultimate intimacy. Her voluptuous mouth parted in a series of little panting moans and he lost all control as his tongue greedily darted and entwined with hers.

She echoed his wild frantic rhythm, his breathing ragged, muscles taut under her hands. Murmured words against her skin, her name, her own voice sounded in mingled confusion as coherent thought flew away.

A shudder ran through him and she clung more tightly, caught in the wild ascent of a dizzying, pulsing spiral as pleasure surged through her in waves of release, feeling all the passion he had held back exploding inside her with a thrill of intensely emotional joy.

He relaxed against her and tears cascaded down her cheeks as she murmured his name, overwhelmed by the profound sense of fulfillment, by the boundless depth of her love.

Quiet filled the room. Gradually her breathing slowed.

The frantic kicking of her heart began to calm. Myles

lifted his flushed face and she pushed the damp strands off his forehead.

"God, you were wonderful," he breathed, a slow, erotic smile lighting his eyes, glazed and sated. "Did I make you feel good, too?"

"Well . . ." she murmured shakily, her hands gliding over his sweat-streaked back. "Maybe not as good as Richie Raven, but you'll do."

"You wretch." Myles rolled over, bringing her with him so that she lay on top and pulled her mouth down to his.

Tiny aftershocks still trembled through her as she luxuriated in the slow sweetness of his kiss. His hands smoothed downward over her damp back in a gentle, caressing motion, to settle possessively on the swell of her hips.

Kate sighed with glowing satisfaction, feeling saturated with happiness. She burrowed against his neck, smiling at the sight of their clothes—his jacket, her dress—scattered heedlessly in their impetuous passion. Then her brow creased in a frown and she lifted her head slightly to look down at him.

"Myles, the party . . ." she murmured.

"What about it?"

His sensuous smile made her tremble inside. Every atom of her being felt alive and vibrant, exquisitely sensitive to his merest touch. No dream or fantasy could compare to this.

"You were the guest of honor. What are people going to say?"

As she spoke the drowsy, desultory words, his eyes moved over her face, focusing distractingly on her mouth.

"I don't give a damn what people say." His hand slid up to her breast, slowly circling his thumb around the nipple, arousing such erotic sensations she could barely think.

"But what about the . . . uh . . . the newspapers getting hold of this?" she whispered dazedly. "You know how they jump to the wrong conclusions."

"But in this case they wouldn't be."

The fingertips of his other hand were slowly tracing down her spine with a shivery sensation that made her squirm against him. Her eyes widened as she felt his body stirring once more.

"Do you regret making love to me?" he murmured provocatively, moving his hips against hers with unmistakable intent.

"Of course not." Her breath caught on a little gasp of pleasure as he trailed a path of moist kisses down the tender skin of her neck.

"Good, because I'm going to do it again." He rolled her a little to one side, his mouth tracing over her collarbone, over the upper swell of her breast.

"Myles . . ." Her shaky warning lacked even the smallest shred of conviction.

"Kate . . ." His muffled voice mimicked her tone and made her laugh, until the teasing stimulation of his mouth turned her laughter into a drawn-out moan of pure delight. The conversation rapidly became distracted and disjointed. Right now she couldn't care less about making sense.

ELEVEN

Kate stirred and opened her eyes to the morning sunlight filtering in through the gauzy curtains, unsure for a moment if she were still dreaming.

It had been no dream. Myles's blond head lay beside her on the lace-trimmed white pillow. She felt the slight friction of his hair-roughened legs entwined with hers under the rumpled sheet. Arching her body in a cat-like stretch, she sighed with pleasure as every achingly sensual moment of their night together came flooding back.

Lovingly her eyes traced his sculpted face, the dark lashes resting on his cheek, the vulnerability of his finely molded mouth. A vulnerability he only betrayed in sleep.

A sudden ache filled her heart. She loved him, but everything was so uncertain between them. No guarantees—that's what he'd said last night, and tomorrow she had to go home.

Home. The word had a hollow sound. A borrowed flat in a city she barely knew. Kate shivered, feeling cold and hopeless. She was in his blood, he said. Had he succeeded now in satisfying his need? Suddenly she didn't want to face whatever would be in his eyes when he awoke.

Carefully edging to the side of the bed, she began swinging her legs over when an arm reached out and caught her around the waist.

"Where do you think you're going?" murmured a sleepy voice behind her. Myles pulled her back, laying her down on the bed and propping himself on one elbow to lean over her. His eyes were drowsy and sensual with desire as he lowered his head to kiss her, long and deep. They pulled apart with a sigh.

"I . . . I can't remember now." How could she ever give up this bliss? "I really should have a shower."

"Good idea." His voice was husky and insinuating. "Let's have a shower."

His provocative smile made her tingle at the thought. "But . . . what about your clothes?" She glanced over at the crumpled, scattered garments on the floor.

"Clothes? Don't be silly. What do we need those for?" He slid his warm body over hers as reason flew away.

"I haven't the faintest idea." She could feel him, hard, against her stomach.

"I have all sorts of plans for us today, and none of them require clothes. Interested?" His eyes were playful and wicked, his smile melting her.

"I could be . . . What do you have in mind?" He made her feel wanton and daring.

"A little game." He took her hands and held them above her head with one of his own, trapping her with his body in voluptuous captivity.

"How do you play it?" His captive squirmed temptingly.

"Well, first you do some of this . . ." His voice was as sinuously suggestive as his touch.

"Mmm . . . yes," she sighed, and arched closer to his mouth.

"And then a little of this . . ." His words were soft against her skin.

She wriggled in delicious torment. "Oh . . . yes. Much more of that . . ." Her voice faded away on a little moan of pleasure.

Later when they lay curled up together, limbs entwined, Myles gently brushed the hair away from her face and gazed thoughtfully into her eyes. "Please don't leave," he murmured.

"I wasn't planning on going anywhere. This is my room, remember?" she teased.

"That's not what I mean . . . I want you to stay with me. Don't go back to London."

For a second her heart stopped, then began to race. Joy exploded inside her. "For how long?" she asked tremulously.

"Till the end of the tour?" His eyes held a trace of uncertainty.

"But that's four months. I can't take that much time off work." But that was just logic talking. Love and desire and hope mingled inside her. She wondered how much he could read in her eyes.

"You can work for me."

"As your paid companion?" She raised her eyebrows and moved her body intimately against his.

He grinned. "If that's what you want. But I had something more legitimate in mind."

She caught her breath in disbelief.

"Would you be interested in writing a book about the tour for me?"

Her heart fell. What a fool she was, even thinking he could have meant something more personal.

"I've decided you may have a point about publicity," he went on. "If it's inevitable, I'd prefer to exercise some control. You've been with the tour from the start. You write well. All in all, you're perfect for the job. In every sense," he added with a soft kiss as he pulled her closer against him.

"Mmm . . . and I love the fringe benefits," she sighed, her mind whirling. "It sounds wonderful, but how can I possibly work it out with Bob?"

"We'll let Tony deal with that." He dismissed the problem, his lips closing possessively over hers again.

Returning the kiss with all the fervent love in her heart, Kate was already persuaded. Four months. Four months before she had to say goodbye. Anything could happen in four months. He might even begin to love her.

Although there had been no promises, no words of love, he needed her and that was a start.

When she went with Myles to the stadium that afternoon Kate sensed in some wonderful unspoken way that he wanted her to be near. And that night she stood in the wings, listening to him sing, so intense, so passionate. She wanted to believe it was all for her.

"Give me your love, tonight . . . I need all of you . . . tonight," he sang, glancing over at Kate, his eyes sending a message of desire to her alone.

In the warm, scented water of the large bathtub, Kate sighed in dreamlike contentment as Myles settled his weight back against her, eyes shut, his head on her breast, her legs encircling his waist.

Between half-closed eyes, the softly lit bathroom of his luxurious suite seemed to shimmer white and gold in the steamy haze. What a glorious way to end the day.

The second concert had been greeted by rapturous acclaim. When he bounded offstage after the encore, Kate had been thrilled by the unfettered pleasure in his smile. Whatever worries he might have had about this tour had clearly been put to rest. But more than that. She wanted to think she was making him happy.

In three days they would be filming the concert at the Mocambo. Three more days in Paris with Myles. Wonderful. Four more months together in North America and the Far East. And then? She rubbed the soap into a silky lather in her hands, refusing to let herself worry about it.

Myles opened his eyes and tilted his head back to look at her for a long, considering moment with a teasing smile.

It didn't take a genius to see that something was on his mind. If she waited for him to speak she could be waiting all night. "Okay . . . what is it?"

His smile broadened at her impatience. "I've just been wondering why you haven't asked me about my father, knowing your irrepressible tendency to snoop."

Kate laughed and flicked water in his face.

"Me? Snoop?"

Where had that come from? She'd longed to ask, but their emotional intimacy was too fragile yet, she couldn't risk it.

"I wouldn't dream of intruding on anyone's privacy," she said lightly, slowly soaping over his hard, muscled chest. Her fingertips slowly trailed circles around his flat nipples, making him squirm.

He grabbed her hands to stop her. "And this from the woman who has such an original approach. Just think, if you'd flunked journalism you could have had a great career in breaking and entering . . . Ouch." He laughed as she gave one nipple a hard tweak.

"That was a vicious thing to say," she rebuked him, then went on artlessly. "Uh, not that I'm interested, but-ummm, . . . why don't you tell me about your father?"

He moved his head further over onto her shoulder and looked up at her with a smug smile.

"Don't bother giving me that 'It was only a matter of time' attitude. You're the one who brought it up!" she said.

He laughed at her exaggeratedly wounded look. Yes, he had brought it up, and he was still wondering why. It had been a long time since he'd felt this relaxed and unguarded. A very long time. Come to think of it, ever since following her into his library he'd found himself acting in ways that confounded every self-protective instinct.

But since that moment when they first made love, when she had wrapped him in her arms, took him into the warm, silken sanctuary of her body, he'd felt a strange happiness that was almost frightening. It went beyond sex, as if some soul-deep longing had been satisfied. But it certainly wasn't something he wanted to analyze. *Let it just happen, take it one day at a time.*

Just looking at her now, her mermaid's eyes glowing with mysterious light, her soft coral mouth begging to be kissed, her skin all pink and flushed from the heat of the bath, he wanted to make love to her all over again. He felt a hunger for her he could never seem to sate. Her very presence in the room brightened the day for him, like this afternoon when she'd breezed in to the Mocambo during rehearsal.

He'd been running through "Dream of Love," one of several songs still in his repertoire from the first album, material he'd begun to tire of performing after ten years. Then he'd seen her pause in the aisle of the old theater and listen, her face rapt and glowing with pleasure. Knowing they held something special for her, he had found himself pouring new emotion into the words he'd written so long ago.

He'd felt tired and jaded for too long until she had come along like a breath of sweet, fresh air, making everything clean and new again.

Kate couldn't read his opaque gray eyes. He had

been gazing up at her in silence for such a long time. Had she made a mistake asking him directly like that? How she hoped he wouldn't go all intense and shuttered. She'd kick herself if she'd ruined the relaxed mood.

He sighed. "My father left us when I was eleven years old. You might say involuntarily." He laughed without the slightest trace of humor and Kate tightened her arms around him in an instinctive gesture of comfort.

"The first my mum heard he'd been selling drugs was the day the police came battering down our front door, looking for the evidence. They were pretty rough with her at first because they thought she was in on it, too." He paused, looking off into some bleak distance. "I'll never forget that look on her face when they took him away. That look of absolute betrayal. How could he do this to us? That was all she kept saying. He'd told her he had a job selling electronic equipment. He was selling all right . . ." Again his harsh laugh. "I never saw the bastard again till the other night. It's funny. After twenty-five years I recognized him instantly. Although he hadn't really changed all that much. Older, more dissipated, that's all. Or maybe it was just that familiar loathing that made it seem like it was only yesterday."

At the despair in his voice she tightened her arms around him, wanting to keep him safe.

"He got ten years for trafficking, got out on parole, and skipped the country. He got off easy. My mum and I didn't. No matter how often we moved, people never let us forget the shame."

Her throat tightened with pain and anger at the injustice of it all. "But you were just a child!" No wonder he had such trouble trusting anyone.

The tenderness of his smile made her heart ache with love for him. Then he surged upward in the water and kissed her cheek. "You're very sweet. I wish I'd met you a long time ago."

His hand curved around her head and brought her mouth down to his. He kissed her, curling his tongue around hers with slow, voluptuous motions. The bath had lulled her into a warm, lazy sensuality, but now she felt the banked fires of desire starting to burn. He seemed to suddenly catch the heat, his tongue exploring her mouth with an explicit, urgent rhythm that made her own need flare deeply inside her. Kate turned toward him until her legs straddled his muscled thigh. She quivered, moving her hips against him, seeking more intimate contact.

He pulled away suddenly and stepped out of the tub. The proud masculinity of his tall, lean, sculpted body took her breath away, made her feel the keen, sharp edge of sexual hunger. He scooped her out of the bath and she looped her arms around his neck, loving the slippery contact of his skin on hers.

"But I'm all wet!" she laughed in protest as he strode through the open doorway, dripping all over the plush white carpeting on his way to the vast, canopied bed.

"That's all right, so am I." His voice was soft, seductive. He dropped her onto the thick duvet, then kneeled by her feet, gently parting her legs as his gaze ran over her, a dark flame burning in his eyes.

Hot, breathless excitement coursed through her. He trailed an exploratory finger slowly up the inside of her knee, sending a tingling heat up her tender inner thigh. She arched voluptuously toward him, offering herself, feeling deliciously desirable. A slight flush edged his high cheekbones as his hot gaze burned into hers.

"We've got all night, Kate." His husky voice caressed her. "Hours and hours. And I intend to take you to the limit and back, give you more pleasure than you ever knew existed. I'll take you to heaven, love . . . Heaven."

* * *

Laden with glossy carrier bags, Kate followed Diana into the elevator.

"That teddy you bought at Lagerfeld is simply delicious. Myles will adore it. Not that you need lingerie to get his attention," she said with a silvery laugh as she pressed the button for the top floor.

Kate studied the toes of her calfskin pumps and felt her cheeks grow slightly warm. "I'm glad you persuaded me to come this morning." She knew she'd been shamefully wrapped up in Myles for the past five days. "Although I really should have been working."

"Oh . . . piffle." Diana flapped an immaculately manicured hand. "Do it this afternoon. I'll just bet Tony hasn't finished with Myles yet. He had scads of contracts and things to go through for the American tour, then they're off to the Mocambo for the filming."

Despite the demands on his time, the past five days with Myles had been like an intoxicating dream. Lunching at little cafes, exploring the famous places, and the unknown Paris of tangled medieval streets.

Most of all she treasured the nights of heady, intoxicating passion, making love with an intensity of need that came from somewhere deep inside, some voice whispering that it might never be like this again.

But she wanted more. She wanted to break through the final barrier. Physically there were no boundaries, no inhibitions, but he still shied away from emotional intimacy. After telling her about his father there had been no more personal revelations. The one time she had inadvertantly mentioned Alison he had gone very quiet, then made such passionate love to her, she had found herself wondering if he were deliberately diverting her.

The Art Nouveau brass doors slid open and Kate stepped out. It was absurd the way her heart beat faster, anticipating the sight of him. It had only been three hours.

"I have the first draft of the article almost finished, but I do still feel a little guilty, though." And not just about the morning spent raiding designer boutiques. There were the stolen hours, the long afternoons of tender, languid caresses.

Diana gave her a warm, amused smile, as if she'd read her mind. "Consider it therapy, then. Shopping beats psychiatry any day of the week, and I should know, I've tried both," she tossed off.

"I don't think I can afford that kind of therapy," Kate countered wryly.

"Oh, but *dahhling*, even when I was poor I loved to shop. I had to become a star just to support my habit." In one extravagant gesture, Diana swept a Hermès bag aloft, like a warrior queen bearing her flag into battle, turned the door handle, and charged into Myles's suite. Kate followed, giggling helplessly.

She noticed Tony first, stacking papers into neat piles on the desk. Brow creased with worry, he looked at Kate as if the sight of her made him deeply uncomfortable.

Myles stood with his back to her. When he turned, her stomach contracted into a tight, hard ball. In the pale, harsh mask of his face, his eyes were glacial.

"What's the matter? What happened?" She approached and put her hand on his arm. He shrugged her off, walking away to the window. "Myles . . . ?" Her eyes fixed on his rigid back, she felt icy-cold with apprehension.

Tony handed her a newspaper clipping.

Millionaire Pop Star Brawls with Drug-dealer Dad screamed the headline. Bylined "Anonymous," flanked by an unflattering photo of Myles, in four paragraphs it painted an ugly, distorted picture of his encounter with his father in Hamburg.

"How on earth did . . ." Kate gasped.

Diana snatched it out of her hand and read it. "What utter crud! Myles, surely you're not letting this bother you? They've said much worse."

"Yes, but I've never been stabbed in the back quite so viciously and thoroughly." His cold eyes never left Kate's face. "You never thought I'd see it. Is that it?" he demanded harshly. "Unfortunately for you, my father would never let an opportunity for cashing in pass him by. He's threatening to sue me for libel, hoping I'll buy him off.

Kate stared in stupefaction.

"Well?" he commanded remorselessly.

"What do you mean?"

"Don't play dumb with me," he raged. "How could you?"

Slowly his meaning penetrated the fog in her brain.

"What's the next installment? A detailed description of what we did in bed?"

"You can't believe I had anything to do with this . . . this abomination!" This couldn't be happening. This must be some sort of nightmare.

"No one else knew about his prison sentence. Only you." His words cut like a knife, his eyes dead, no spark of feeling left, just barely controlled anger.

"Oh, Myles, you can't be serious, Kate would never—"

"Stay out of this, Diana," Myles cut her off mercilessly.

How could he? How could he think this of her? Kate felt as if she'd been plunged into hell. She couldn't speak, couldn't move, for the pain knifing through her. Myles's face dissolved as her eyes filled with angry tears. Her gaze flew desperately from him to Tony, looking grave and sad. Not him, too?

"After everything that's happened between us, I can't believe you'd think me capable of something like that!'' Kate sobbed out. Diana moved closer, putting a protective arm around her shoulder.

"Maybe you're cleverer than I thought," Myles went on, "worming your way into my bed. Dangling your favors in front of my nose, then whisking them away, getting me so frustrated I'd forget you're a reporter and start trusting you."

Parading their private moments in front of the others was the final humiliation.

"You . . . son of a bitch!" She stepped toward him. "If I were a man I'd smash you right in your arrogant face!"

"If you were a man, your dirty little scheme would never have worked in the first place, would it?"

It didn't make sense. Something else was bothering him. "What are you really angry about, Myles? You can't believe I sold that article."

"Maybe you didn't actually sell it, but you probably couldn't resist sharing such a little gem with one of your reporter friends down at the magazine."

"Oh, yes . . . and we had a damn good laugh about it, too. There! Does that make you feel better? You're a coward, Myles." She'd finally figured it out. "You found yourself getting in too deep, and instead of talking to me about it honestly, you're using this convenient escape."

"Don't give me any of your women's magazine, pop-culture psychology."

"Oh, yes, that's typical. Hide behind that sneering contempt. You do it so well, but it doesn't fool me for a second. I won't be your scapegoat because you're afraid of life."

She pushed hard on his chest and he reeled backward as she went for the door, past the shocked faces of Tony and Diana, who stood frozen to the spot like statues.

"Just a minute, I'm not finished with you yet."
Myles followed her and grabbed her arm.

"Maybe not, but I'm finished with you." She
wrenched out of his grasp.

"Just a minute," Diana called out to her.

"Don't try to stop me." It took a superhuman effort
to keep her voice from cracking.

"Stop you? I'm coming with you." Kate turned to
her for a second, but Diana was looking at Myles and
Tony. "I hope you're both satisfied."

Not wanting to hear any more, she ran down the
corridor to her room and heard Diana following. Once
there, Kate threw herself on the bed, torn by
wrenching, hiccuping sobs. The door closed and she
felt Diana sit down on the bed beside her and stroke
her hair in a slow, soothing motion.

"There, there . . . It's not the end of the world. Give
Myles time and he'll be the first one to admit he behaved like a swine. He was hurt and lashing out because what you said was true, and deep down inside he
knows it. Believe me, I know Myles. He does care."

"I don't think so," Kate sobbed unevenly. "How
can he when he doesn't even trust me?"

"You and Myles need to talk about this when you've
both calmed down. I know it looks very black, but you
can work it out."

The other woman's soothing optimism was almost
drowned out by her tortured weeping.

Diana stayed with her until the storm had passed.
Finally convincing Kate to get some rest, she left,
promising to return later. When the door closed behind
her, Kate rolled onto her back and stared up at the
ornately plastered ceiling through burning eyes.

All her strength and anger had deserted her. *Myles,
I love you. Why did you do this to us?* The thought
revolved endlessly as she lay there, motionless and

numb. But nothing could dull the agony of her breaking heart.

The birds in the enclosed courtyard sang through the fresh green leaves of early summer, but Kate was deaf and blind to everything. Inside she felt dead. It was over.

She'd been hoping someday he'd be able to say he loved her, but how could those words mean anything without trust?

Pulling out her suitcase, she shoved her clothes in carelessly. Half her things were still in his room. It didn't matter. Nothing mattered anymore.

She had such hopes for the future, and in one fell swoop he had destroyed them all. The only thought her mind could fix on was to get away, escape everything as quickly as possible.

Sitting in the lounge at Orly Airport an hour later waiting to board, over the gabbling voices of the other passengers, she heard a familiar voice singing far above. Wildly she looked around for the source. Over the speakers came a Paris radio station playing the number-one hit in Europe.

"Give me back my stolen dreams,
I need the mercy I see in your eyes.
Please don't give me modern love
I don't need those empty lies."

He would follow her everywhere. There would be no escape from heartbreak.

TWELVE

Did shell-shock victims feel like this? Walking around, talking, working, going through the motions of daily life, while inside there was nothing left.

Kate sat at her desk, staring sightlessly out the window and across the road at the green trees, barely stirring in the hot July breeze. Never in her life had she felt so desolately alone. Being back in London, she had no one to cling onto. No family, no real friends.

She sighed heavily and turned back to the keyboard. At least the worst was over. Finishing the article had been torture, like tearing open her wounded heart all over again, but she had done it. Bob had the first draft now.

Thank goodness he had granted her request for two weeks off and let her work at home. Pleading the flu might have been a cowardly excuse, but her pale, drawn face and red-rimmed eyes betrayed an abject misery that went soul deep.

After two weeks she should have got a grip on herself, stopped crying every time she heard his voice on the radio. Now she just left it switched off.

Kate picked up the photo lying on her desk, the one

she had taken on that crazy impulse in the stands at Düsseldorf. He looked so completely disarmed and natural, the real man she had fallen in love with. The first time she saw it she'd laughed. Now each compulsive glance gave her a crushing pain in her heart.

But she had to ignore the pain. There was nothing left now but her work, so she'd better do a damn good job of it. She stared at the screen and tried to compose another sentence.

Why couldn't he just have let it happen between them? The question kept tormenting her. She would never have pushed him, or burdened him with expectations. Only stay with him, hoping he would come to realize that loving was not such a doomed, painful thing.

Days might be hell, but nights were intolerable. Lying in her solitary bed feeling icy-cold, she longed for his body nestled close to hers, his arms around her. The need for him was in her blood like a tropical fever that could never be cured.

She shook herself out of her trance, realizing the phone had been ringing insistently. It was Bob.

"You're going to the Hammersmith show tonight," he barked peremptorily. "I've got the tickets here at the office."

Kate's heart turned over, but she swallowed hard and forced her voice to sound normal. "But the article's done. It was only supposed to cover Europe."

She looked at the picture in her trembling hand and knew how desperately she longed to see him, and how much it would hurt.

"This isn't a major rewrite, don't panic," Bob said impatiently. "But after the way it's gone in Europe, this London date looks like being a triumphant homecoming. You know, the usual tripe. Local boy makes good, fades, then makes a comeback." He sounded more world-weary than usual this morning. "It'll make a good tie-off."

He wouldn't relent, and her panic-stricken mind couldn't come up with an excuse. After Bob rang off, she put down the phone in a daze.

Tonight. The concert was tonight. She'd have to see him, have to listen to him, knowing he was lost to her. The thought was unbearable.

Even though Kate deliberately arrived at the old Hammersmith Odeon at the last minute, fans still crowded the pavement haggling for the few remaining tickets. As she walked through the door, the oppressive heat of the packed house hit her in the face. In the rising buzz of the crowd she could feel that familiar sense of electric anticipation.

She looked around for her seat in the tenth row, wishing they'd hurry up and turn down the house lights. She *had* to be there, but she dreaded seeing a familiar face, being made to endure questions and speculation.

"Kate! . . . Hello there."

After a momentary panic, she saw with profound relief it was only Eva, the junior secretary who had won the draw for the other complimentary ticket. Edging through the row, Kate took her seat beside the excited girl.

"I've never seen him in concert before, but I love his videos!" she burbled. "I wonder if he looks the same? I think he's so gorgeous! Don't you think he's gorgeous?"

She went on and on, completely unaware that Kate's polite smile was becoming more and more brittle. Finally her patience snapped.

"For God's sake, stop acting like a simpering idiot and get a grip on yourself!"

Eva's mouth hung open in an offended stare.

"Witch," she muttered under her breath. But it stopped her.

Kate felt instant remorse for her unthinking rudeness. It wasn't Eva's fault. She must be sure to make it up to the poor girl tomorrow. But right now she could only cross her arms tightly over her body and fight down the rising anguish inside.

Finally the lights dimmed and a voice offstage made the familiar introduction. The band slammed into "Dance with me," and suddenly there he was, pouring out an energetic, powerful show.

How could he look the same? How could he be so animated, so engaging, so absolutely unchanged, when she felt like she'd been dragged through hell and back? Had it meant that little that he could recover so quickly?

Kate sat dazed in a cocoon of unreality, while all around her the crowd was going wild, Eva bouncing up and down in her seat in ecstasies.

And up there, bathed in the golden halo of the spotlight, stood the man she loved beyond anything else in the world. The man who had shared with her the sweetest intimacy, the most profound passion she'd ever known.

At least, that's how it had been for her. It had been a delusion to think their interlude had been any different from the affairs he'd had before. Once again he'd walked away unscathed.

Just one of the crowd. How could she have let herself believe anything different? Sick with misery, she sat inert through the familiar repertoire. Finally the music rose to a crescendo and with a crash of chords he yelled out, "Good night," and the stage went black.

Roaring and stamping, the crowd called for an encore, until Kate thought the old theater would come tumbling down around their ears. A lone spot picked out the microphone stand and Myles stepped into the circle of light, to an answering roar of approval from the audience.

"This is for you," he said quietly, his voice husky and a little strained. He seemed to look straight at her. She held her breath for a moment, then let it out in a rush. *Stop deluding yourself. It's only your imagination.*

But she edged forward in her seat as, alone with only an acoustic guitar, he began playing an unfamiliar tune and breaking her heart all over again.

His voice echoed out across the hushed theater, full of emotion, edged with despair. Everyone held their breath.

> *I could be the lover You've been waiting for.*
> *Or I could ruin everythinq for you.*
> *I dream every night of all our wasted words*
> *Doesn't matter what I do*
> *Someone let love into my heart*
> *You.''*

The song ended, and for a brief suspended moment silence reigned. Then came a thundering torrent of applause, yelling, screaming. All around, little flickering points of light sprang up in the universal gesture of approval. Kate sat, stunned, while the crowd erupted around her.

Those words she'd read in Hamburg . . . the anguish behind the lyrics. How could he write that if she didn't mean anything to him? But, no. She remembered asking him how he could exploit his emotions in his songs, thinking of the album after Alison's death. In her head Myles's voice echoed clearly: "Because it sells records."

The house lights went up, but the audience didn't stop cheering, hoping for another encore. Overcome,

Kate buried her face in her hands and realized her cheeks were wet with tears. She had to get out. Pushing her way through the jumping, screaming throng to the aisle, she began running for the exit. Through the noise she thought she heard her name.

A hand shot out and grabbed her arm in a viselike grip. Turning, she saw the florid face of Andy Sprye.

"Myles wants to see you backstage."

"What does he want?" Her heart crashed against her ribs, but she deliberately quashed the flicker of hope springing up inside.

"I don't know. You'll have to talk to him yourself."

"Give your boss a message." Her anguish made her defiant. "If he wants to see me, he knows where I am."

"Sorry. I've got my orders." He started hauling her down the aisle as Kate protested furiously. The crowd surged past, ignoring the little drama going on in their midst.

"Let go of me, you big ox!" She aimed a swift kick at his shins, and missed. He stopped and turned to her with a surprisingly kindly look of patience.

"Look, Kate, do you want me to lose my job? I'm just doing as I was told."

He was right, why take it out on him. Her anger burned white-hot now. She'd reserve her venom for his high-handed boss and his imperious summonses.

"All right." She sniffed rebelliously. "I'll see him, but he'll be sorry."

They made their way through narrow backstage corridors to Myles's dressing room, Kate's face set in a mutinous scowl, passing the usual knots of hangers-on. She knew she looked awful. Her simple white cotton dress hung loosely, revealing her loss of weight and only accentuating her pallor, but she didn't care.

Andy knocked on the door, and from inside she heard

Myles tell him to enter. He pulled out a large white handkerchief from his pocket and thrust it at Kate.

"Here. You don't want him seeing you like that," he winked. She wiped her eyes, blew her nose, and handed the handkerchief back to him. He looked at the crumpled ball in distaste, stuffed it in his pocket, and walked away.

Kate opened the door. Her heart lurched with a mixture of love and hurt and anger.

Emerging from what she assumed to be the bathroom, Myles had his face buried in a towel. As he lowered it his gaze slid over her, as cool and impersonal as on that first day in his library.

"Come on in and close the door." His voice matched his look. Did she only imagine that his fine-boned features looked a little drawn, the lines beside his mouth a little deeper?

Kate hovered on the brink of telling him to go to hell. Instead she did as he said, still wondering what he wanted. His complete indifference killed any hope Andy's message had aroused.

"I've just received the first draft of your article. It's not bad . . . but I've changed my mind. I'm withdrawing my approval." He spoke as coolly as if they were discussing the weather, then walked behind a cream-colored screen set in the corner of the room.

Kate stood openmouthed for a moment in disbelief before her fury exploded.

"What do mean you're withdrawing your approval?"

She strode in after him and stopped abruptly at the sight of him taking off his damp shirt. Quelling her instinctive physical reaction to the smooth-muscled, golden flesh of his chest took conscious effort. A vividly painful memory flashed through her mind, of making love with him that last morning in Paris. Her lips still remembered the taste of his skin. But she wouldn't let it deflect her from her purpose.

"I *said*, what do mean, withdrawing your approval?" she demanded again.

He turned his back to her, slipping on a fresh white shirt. "That was the agreement, wasn't it?" he said over his shoulder, maddeningly calm and controlled. "That I'd have final veto."

"I know what you're doing, Myles Hunter." She walked around to confront him, jabbing him in the chest with her finger. "You're just trying to punish me. *I* get to be the whipping boy. *I'm* the one who has to pay for the sins of my whole damn profession, right?"

He gave no apparent response to her rage. Not a flicker of anger or irritation showed in his gray eyes as he buttoned his shirt and looped a black silk tie around his neck. She couldn't stand it. His continued impassivity made her boil.

He began calmly knotting his tie and walked out from behind the screen over to a full-length mirror beside the dressing table, where he adjusted the knot more precisely while Kate stormed on.

"Well, I won't let you sabotage my career." She grabbed the damp towel from the top of the screen and hurled it at him. It hit his back and dropped to the floor.

He paused for a moment in the minute correction of his attire, looking calmly down at the towel, then back to Kate.

"Stop being so dramatic," he said, unruffled.

"It's that damn story about your father, isn't it? Well, just for the record, I didn't write it!" In impotent fury she stamped her foot and kicked at the wardrobe case beside the table. Pain shot through her stubbed toe as she stifled an exclamation.

Myles raised an eyebrow at her impassioned outburst, the corner of his mouth quirked as if with the effort of concealing a grin. But when he spoke his voice held the same cool, impassive tone.

"It's got nothing to do with the story." He sat down on the dressing-table chair and began pulling on soft black leather shoes. "As a matter of fact, I found out *my father*," his voice hardened with contempt at the words, "sold that story, painting himself in the worst possible light so he could turn around and soak me for all he could get." He finished tying his shoes and looked up at her with a mixture of disgust and impatience.

"So why?" she demanded. "Why are you doing this?"

He stood up and shrugged. "I just changed my mind. That's all." He picked up the jacket of his black suit and slid his arms into the sleeves.

"You bastard!" She wanted to smash that cool veneer, make him hurt. "It's so easy for you, isn't it, Myles? You can snap your fingers and ruin my career without a second thought. You're just an unfeeling, selfish, supercilious, conceited, sarcastic swine!"

"Stop trying to impress me with your vocabulary, Kate."

This bored impatience was the final insult. She turned away in impotent frustration. She couldn't reach him, couldn't elicit even a flicker of emotion.

"Of course, there is one way to change my mind about all this."

She closed her eyes, steeling herself for whatever fresh humiliation he had in store. "What?"

"You could marry me." His simple words had the impact of an atom bomb in the quiet room.

She whirled around in disbelief. The cool detachment had gone, replaced by a look of such burning intensity it made her tremble.

"What did you say?" She heard the words, but her numbed mind couldn't immediately register them.

"I asked you to marry me." He stepped toward her and held his breath.

She stood looking at him, transfixed. He couldn't tell what was going on in her mind. Had he been wrong? Could she still care? God knows he hadn't given her any reason to go on caring. She was right, he *was* a coward. He couldn't just come right out out with it the minute he saw her. He'd kept up that silly charade to gauge her reactions. If she'd been completely apathetic he'd have known it was too late.

He ran a shaking hand through his hair. His whole future was at stake here. "Kate, can you ever forgive me?"

With a little cry, she launched herself at him, almost sending him off balance, and he felt an insanely wonderful sense of homecoming as her arms closed around him and her lips met his. He didn't deserve this sort of happiness, but he had to thank God.

Clinging tightly to her in a deep, searching kiss, he felt her trembling in his arms. Her mouth opened to his like a flower to the rain, thirsty and elemental. His hands moved over her body in a fever of possession. Would he ever be able to satisfy the desperate hunger inside him?

The same hunger flooded through Kate, released like a frozen river overflowing its banks in the passionate turbulence of spring. She wanted to spend eternity in his arms. All the pain and despair and loneliness of the past two weeks sought healing in that kiss.

He lifted his face from her and she could see what a strain it had been for him keeping up the cool facade. With a sigh he buried his face against the curve of her neck. Wanting to soothe the tension she could still feel in his body, she drifted her hands through his hair.

"You were absolutely right, Kate. All those things you said to me in Paris were true. In my heart I knew you couldn't have written that article, or have had anything to do with it. I *did* push you away, because I didn't want to need you. I was afraid of losing control of my life by giving you the power to hurt me."

He sat in the chair and pulled her onto his lap. She pressed her lips gently to his forehead. Right now she didn't need any reasons, only the wonderful intoxication of being cradled in his arms, but it was clearly important to Myles.

"Go on," she murmured.

"But what frightened me most was the realization I couldn't contemplate life without you."

"How long did it take you to discover that?" she smiled.

"As soon as you left." His voice sounded agonized. "For the first time I had to face up to the past and then put it behind me. When I did, I realized that the only thing that could make me happy was to spend the rest of my life with you. But I had to convince myself that I deserved you, after everything I had done."

"Is that why you never came looking for me?"

"No . . . because it didn't take that long to convince myself."

"I see you haven't lost your humility." She gave him a playful jab in the ribs and he retaliated by kissing her. After a moment he continued.

"I did try to find you. I couldn't get away, but I kept calling that damn magazine. No one would give me your address or phone number. They would only tell me you were away sick. I was out of my mind with worry." He shuddered and his arms tightened around her. "Then finally Diana suggested I send a couple of passes, with specific instructions that you attend. I'm not ashamed to admit I leaned on your editor pretty heavily to ensure that. When I looked out beforehand and saw that other girl I thought you couldn't have loved me, you were so angry and disgusted you couldn't stand to see me. Then you arrived . . ."

She stopped him with her mouth, bending her head

to kiss his firm, responsive lips with searing passion. They finally pulled apart, a little breathless. Distracted, Myles's gaze burned into her, but with a deep breath he single-mindedly pursued his point.

"Now, you still haven't answered my question, and if you say no comment, I really will cancel the article, and strangle you, to boot."

"What was the question again?" As if she could have forgotten.

"Kate . . ." His voice rang with an unspoken threat.

Kate laughed, and knew for once she would be incapable of keeping him in suspense. "You know I'll marry you, but are you sure it's what you want?" She sobered, becoming uncertain and earnest. "Because it would break my heart if you change your mind."

A shadow crossed his face. "I know I've hurt you, Kate, but I swear I'll never hurt you again." His arms tightened around her. "But you have to know what you're letting yourself in for, marrying me. I have to tell you about Alison."

"You don't have to tell me anything about her. It's got nothing to do with us."

"But I do. I want to explain to you, so that we can start our life together fresh, with no secrets between us. Alison's death wasn't accidental. She committed suicide," he said bluntly, "and it was my fault."

Kate gasped at the baldness of his flat, unemotional statement.

"She was a manic-depressive with suicidal tendencies, but I didn't discover that till after we were married. At first I thought her paranoia and jealousy were just insecurity. I laughed it off and told her she had nothing to worry about, but she'd go into these hysterical rages and accuse me of imaginary affairs . . ." He paused, his gaze becoming more intense. "I was faithful to my wife until the day she died."

Kate leaned down and kissed him, wanting to erase the pain and bitterness she saw in his eyes.

"But Alison refused to trust me. She took every tabloid story as gospel truth. Eventually she killed my love for her, until only pity remained. Our marriage was basically over. Yet how could I leave her when she needed me? Eventually she became frighteningly self-destructive, until one day she got into her car and drove it off a bridge. In her note she said I didn't love her, that I had no time for her because of my career," his voice broke with emotion, "and it was all true."

"Myles, darling." Kate pulled him close. "This is what you've been blaming yourself for all these years?"

"Don't you understand? If I'd really loved her, I would have been there all the time."

"What do you mean? Giving up your life for her?" Kate held his face in her hands. "It wouldn't have made any difference. You know that, don't you?"

"The point is, with Alison I was far too involved in my career. I still am, but I'd give it all up for you if you wanted me to, because I've realized my success means nothing to me without you to share it."

"I'd never ask that of you," Kate said tremulously, overwhelmed by what he was confessing.

"You've reaffirmed my faith in myself, in my capacity to truly love, which I seriously doubted. You've made a believer of me."

"How?"

"You know that old cliché, love conquers all?" His smile faded as that haunted look clouded his eyes. "But it won't be easy, Kate. Being in the public eye puts a strain on a relationship, no matter how strong."

"I can take a lot. I'm pretty tough."

"I know. That's what I admire about you."

"And I'd never hurt you, Myles," Kate said passionately.

"I know that, too." The hand stroking her cheek

shook slightly. "You know, right from the moment we first met, you stirred something inside me."

"I thought you couldn't stand me!"

"I'm very good at hiding my feelings," he said with a wry smile. "Besides, I resented like hell feeling that way about a reporter, of all people. I knew I'd let you come, I knew I'd go after you, and I knew you'd disturb my neatly ordered, empty life. I just had no idea how much you'd disturb it."

"So in Frankfurt you thought you'd get me out of your system."

"Yes . . . that's when I realized my emotions were getting much too involved."

"Your emotions? I thought it was my emotions you were so worried about!"

He laughed, shaking his head. "Poor Kate, always my scapegoat."

Then his expression changed as his eyes focused on her lips. Taking her face in his hands, his mouth found hers again, kissing her deeply, intimately. Her hand unfastened a shirt button and slid beneath to feel the smooth, familiar skin. With difficulty Kate paused.

"So . . . what *exactly* are you trying to tell me?" she said breathlessly, wanting him to say it without her help.

"You really want to make this difficult for me, don't you?" His eyes clouded with emotion. "I suppose I find it hard to put my feelings into words."

"Except in a song," she smiled. "Please try . . ."

"I love you, Kate." He looked into her eyes and Kate held her breath in wonderment. All the barriers were gone. For the first time she felt as if she were looking into his soul. "I want to spend the rest of my life with you, making up for all the hurt and pain I've caused you. I . . ."

Overwhelmed with intense happiness, Kate didn't wait to hear anymore. Her mouth came down hard on his in a hungry, passionate outpouring of love. Lips parting to each other, tongues tasting, entwining in a hot, deep kiss of such recklessly greedy abandon it took her breath away.

Without warning the door burst open and Diana flew in, followed by a sheepish Tony.

"Well! I must say it took you long enough. Do you know how difficult it is listening at keyholes? It's back breaking. Honestly, darling, you *are* long-winded."

Kate looked up at Diana and Tony, and a warm feeling of belonging swept over her. These people were the closest thing to family that Myles had, and now they were her family, too.

"Diana, do shut up," Myles said with indulgent patience. "And lock the door on your way out," he added with a wickedly provocative smile that was for Kate alone.

EPILOGUE

Kate lay in luxurious contentment, soft sand beneath her towel, the Caribbean sun warming her bare skin as she listened with closed eyes to the waves washing in a few feet away.

It had been a beautiful wedding. Maggie cried, her mother cried, Diana cried. It had been perfect. After the initial surprise of their announcement, Myles had brought everyone over to stay for a few days before the ceremony.

Her parents worried that they were rushing things, but in his inimitable way he charmed them all, and she knew he'd laid their fears to rest. It touched her to realize how important it was for Myles to be accepted by her family.

And now here they were, spending a brief honeymoon at his island home before the American tour began. Kate rolled over onto her stomach and propped her head on her hands to watch Myles come walking up the beach toward her from the house.

The sun had lightened his blond hair to the color of ripe wheat and tanned his firm body a rich golden brown, shown off to advantage by the brief black swimsuit. Just looking at him made her heart beat faster with desire in the intoxicating knowledge that he belonged to her.

Even now, she still wasn't quite used to the idea of being his wife. He dropped down beside her, grinning boyishly as she reached up to ruffle his hair. The sultry, intimate expression in his eyes made her heart turn over.

He no longer had that haunted look. It had been replaced by a deep contentment, a calm happiness she had never seen in him before, a reflection of her own sense of fulfillment and belonging.

She pulled him toward her and kissed him, tasting the warmth of his lips. Once again she felt the immediate response burgeoning inside her. Always that same fire between them, that magic.

Myles groaned softly and pushed himself away from her, then got to his feet and held out a hand. His movements were languid, his eyes still smoldering with promise. She put her hand in his and allowed him to pull her up. Slowly he began backing toward the water, drawing her along with him, his gaze locked on hers.

He watched her face, fascinated by her beautiful mouth curving in a smile, her damp hair dark and glossy in the sunshine. Her soft, smooth skin had turned the color of honey, giving her eyes the same intense aqua-green hue as the Caribbean. Droplets of water clinging to her face shimmered in the light, but it was her expression that captivated him, that radiance that he knew shone for him alone.

His eyes skimmed down her body, over the low, tantalizing scoop of the white tank suit. He couldn't stop himself from touching and reached for her with the other hand, allowing it to trace the swell of her breast, slide into the curve of her slender waist, then around the high-cut leg exposing her tanned thighs to cup her firm bottom.

The silky warm water lapped against his ankles as he kept on going, drawing her in deeper with him. As it crept up past his waist he leaned back into it and pulled her on top of him.

With a soft laugh she surged against him, wrapping her arms around his neck. Her hips moved against his and he felt the sweet ache of his body's response as the water closed over his head.

He surfaced and knelt on the soft sand, waves lapping shoulder-high. Kate still clung to him, and he lifted her until she straddled his lap, her arms wrapped around his neck. He couldn't keep his hands from caressing her.

For a second he almost felt afraid. Everything was too perfect. But the brief flare of anxiety vanished as he gazed back into her sea-green eyes so full of love. She made him feel safe, in a way he had never felt before. The future no longer loomed ahead, bleak and empty. Now when he looked into the future he saw Kate and knew it would be wonderful.

"That was Tony on the phone."

Kate leaned forward and started to nuzzle his earlobe. "Uh huh."

Her warm mouth set off a wild tingling inside him as he closed his eyes and let his head fall back a little. Her slightest touch was enough to arouse him.

She pulled back a little. "What did Tony have to say?"

He smiled at himself. Right now he just wanted to carry her up onto the beach and make love to her in the warm sand. After all these weeks of being together he still wanted her all the time. A look, a gesture, that was all it took from her to set him on fire.

"Myles?"

Suddenly he felt overwhelmed by a sense of complete and utter happiness, a feeling he couldn't ever remember before. He surged to his feet, Kate still clinging to his neck, her legs wrapped around his waist, and twirled her around, sending a fan of spray sparkling in the brilliant sunshine.

The water foamed and splashed around his knees as he came to a stop. Until this moment he'd never realized how sweet the feeling of success could be. But it would never have felt so sweet without this woman in his arms. "The album just went double platinum in Japan and Australia."

Kate gasped, then tightened her arms around his neck, laughing. "Oh, Myles, that's just wonderful. I knew it would."

"How could you know?"

"Because *I* like it."

He threw back his head and laughed. "And, of course, everyone in the world has to be led by your superior taste."

She struggled out of his arms and pushed him at the same time so that he toppled backward, still laughing as he fell to the soft, wet sand, the velvety warm water lapping at his chest. Before he could move she had straddled him and grabbed his wrists to pin his arms above his head. He looked up at her leaning over him, her dark hair tumbled and damp around her face, her eyes sparkling with mock ferocity.

"You can laugh, but I'll have you know I single-handedly contributed to your wealth over the years. The albums. The concert tickets. My God, the T-shirts alone add up to a fortune! When I was seventeen I slept with you every night."

He grinned. "I know—the posters." The delicious warmth of her against his belly was driving him crazy. He moved beneath her, trying to make her move down over his hips, wanting her to feel what she did to him.

"How did you know?" Kate's eyes widened, then realization dawned.

"Maggie," they both said at the same time, Kate in exasperation, Myles echoing in amused confirmation.

She shook her head. "I'll never forget your first concert in Toronto. I was standing right at the barrier, as close as I ever got. I had tears running down my face for the entire two hours."

"Oh, so you were the one." He smiled up at her.

"You never even looked at me."

Something in her wistful smile made him go still. He reached up, curving his hand around the nape of her neck, slowly pulling her closer to him until he murmured against her lips, "I wish I had," before he parted them with his tongue and kissed her.

Suddenly a wave washed over him, pulling them apart. He sat up and pushed the streaming hair off his face to see Kate doing the same. He caught her eye and smiled, and the knowing curve of her lips told him she had read his unspoken message. They rose at the same time. He put his arm around her shoulders and felt her arm slip instinctively around his waist as they slowly waded out onto the sand.

He looked down at her. "Tony told me that we're adding more dates in Asia and Australia. The tour will be going at least another eight months. I want you to be with me. I know that's a long time to take away from your work, but let's find some way of getting around that. I don't want us to be separated right now." He stroked her shoulder.

"We're not going to be separated. I had every intention of coming on this tour just to keep an eye on you." She gave him a saucy look and met his indulgent smile.

"Actually Tony also suggested you might want to get started on the book we talked about. And you won't be alone. Diana sends her love and has threatened to join us in New York."

Kate squeezed him tighter. "That's great! We'll have a lot of fun. And I *love* the idea of doing the book.

I've already spoken to Bob and I've told him I want to work freelance from now on and it looks like I've just got my first job.''

"How did he take that?"

"Oh, he's quite happy with the plan."

Okay, so maybe happy was not the right word. In fact Bob had skewered her with a skeptical look and snorted, "Happens every time. Give a woman reporter the job and next thing you know she's hooked the poor blighter. I suppose the next step will be quitting altogether when the baby comes along." And this was all at the wedding reception. She had to smile at the recollection. Bob would never change.

They strolled past her blanket, still lying on the beach. Never mind, she'd get it later. Ahead, the white stucco house lay hidden behind tall, graceful palms bending in the tradewinds.

"So I guess being written by my biggest fan, this book will make me look pretty good, huh? Redeem my debauched character and paint me well nigh a saint.''

"Oh, no, I believe in telling the truth, remember?"
She tilted her head up to him with a teasing smirk as they stepped onto the paved terrace that wrapped around the house.

Shaded by the swaying palms, tropical flowers cascaded from massive terra cotta pots to blaze in all their lush glory against the white walls of the house and send a shower of petals to the tiles with every stray breath of air.

"Wretch," he murmured, his voice soft and intimate, as he opened the door that led off the terrace directly into their bedroom. She walked past him into the room, feeling his eyes burning over her, and caught the slow smile on his lips as he closed the door.

She paused by the window. The white gauze curtain billowed up for a moment with a sudden gust of ocean breeze, hiding Myles from her sight for a moment. As it drifted back into place they moved toward each other and began to slowly peel off the other's damp swimsuit.

It was a miracle, a constant source of wonder to her, the way they could still never get enough of each other, familiarity only intensifying the pleasure of their love-making and Myles's boundless, imaginative passion. Kate smiled into his eyes as he laid her down on the crisp white sheets, loving him so intensely, it went beyond words.

"Penny for your thoughts . . ." he said, his voice husky with desire. He leaned up on his elbow beside her, slowly smoothing her hair away from her face.

"You asked me that once before," she rolled on her side to face him, "in Brussels, as I recall. I've been thinking about the same thing . . . you."

"That's not what you said then."

"Of course not, how could I tell you I was lusting after you." With a wicked little smile of anticipation, she reached around and caressed the firm, smooth flesh of his buttocks. She saw his eyes darkening with passion.

"If that's the case, why didn't you take me up on my invitation to play?" he asked, returning the favor.

"If you were so worried about me disturbing your peace of mind, why did you invite me?"

"I suppose I thought reducing it to that meaningless level would make it easier to handle." Cupping her silken flesh, he pulled her hips closer to his so that they were almost touching.

"But I wouldn't cooperate, so you had to console yourself with Lise Fremont." She gave him a resounding slap where her hand had been caressing a moment before.

"Ouch," he yelped, then began to laugh. "For your information I wasn't able to interest myself in anyone after I met you." He gave a long-suffering sigh. "Although, God knows I tried."

"Yes, I noticed." Kate's eyes narrowed in mock jealousy. "I hope you realize the Lise Fremont days are over."

She rubbed the area she had smacked with delicious slowness, feeling the gratifying response of his body to her touch. "Because I have to warn you, I'm never going to let you go. I'm not very modern about love."

"And I'd better not ever catch you flirting with the likes of Adam Benedict, or I'll . . ."

"Or you'll what?" she challenged, running her caressing fingers over his hard arousal.

With a gasp, he rolled her over onto her back and covered her body with his. "I'll tell you tomorrow . . . and tomorrow . . . and tomorrow . . ."

SHARE THE FUN . . .
SHARE YOUR NEW-FOUND TREASURE!!

You don't want to let your new books out of your sight?
That's okay. Your friends can get their own. Order below.

No. 110 BEGINNINGS by Laura Phillips
Abby had her future completely mapped out—until Matt showed up.

No. 111 CALIFORNIA MAN by Carole Dean
Quinn had the Midas touch in business but Emily was another story.

No. 112 MAD HATTER by Georgia Helm
Sara returns home and is about to make a deal with the man called Devil!

No. 113 I'LL BE HOME by Judy Christenberry
It's the holidays and Lisa and Ryan exchange the greatest gift of all.

No. 114 IMPOSSIBLE MATCH by Becky Barker
As Tyler falls in love with Chantel, it gets harder to keep his secret.

No. 115 IRON AND LACE by Nadine Miller
Shayna was not about to give an inch where Joshua was concerned!

No. 116 IVORY LIES by Carol Cail
April makes Semi a very unusual proposition and it backfires on them.

----

knew existed. I'll take you to heaven, too! Heaven."